LUCY JANE
AND THE
RUSSIAN BALLET

Also by Susan Hampshire

LUCY JANE AT THE BALLET
LUCY JANE ON TELEVISION
LUCY JANE AND THE
DANCING COMPETITION

SUSAN HAMPSHIRE

LUCY JANE
AND THE
RUSSIAN
BALLET

Illustrated by Honey de Lacey

METHUEN

My grateful thanks to Honey de Lacey for her lovely
warm drawings of Lucy Jane and company. Many thanks to
Ros Logan for typing and retyping the book and Emma Rees
for typing the manuscript. Last but never least, again a million
thanks to Miriam Hodgson whose encouragement and kindness
and tireless guidance keeps Lucy Jane going from book to book.

For my great-niece GRACE and all children with dreams

First published in Great Britain 1993
by Methuen Children's Books
an imprint of Reed Consumer Books Limited
Michelin House, 81 Fulham Road, London SW36RB
and Auckland, Melbourne, Singapore and Toronto

ISBN 0 416 18867 2

Printed in England by Clays Ltd, St Ives plc

A CIP catalogue record for this book is available at the
British Library

Contents

Chapter 1   The Announcement   7

Chapter 2   Swan Lake   17

Chapter 3   The Surprise   26

Chapter 4   The Audition   39

Chapter 5   The Result   47

Chapter 6   The New Life   55

Chapter 7   'My little star'   65

Chapter 8   'Getting to Know You'   76

Chapter 9   Moscow   87

Chapter 10   Lucy's Decision   99

1

The Announcement

'Guess what?' Lucy Jane said excitedly, jumping up and down on the kitchen tiles waving a piece of paper. 'Some girls may be chosen to go and train in Russia in the summer holidays.'

Mrs Tadworth stopped buttering the bread.

'Russia?' She was amazed.

'Yes, Russia,' her daughter said again. 'To study at the Hirkov Ballet School with Madame Something-or-other,' Lucy Jane explained, quite pink in the cheeks.

'I really want to go, Mummy,' Lucy Jane pleaded. 'I know you'd have to pay and Granny would be upset if I don't go to Scotland for the holidays, but . . .' She suddenly stopped and looked at her feet. She stretched her right foot to the side and pointed her toe, then she swished it back and forth across the kitchen tiles.

'I know I wear glasses,' Lucy Jane continued with difficulty, still looking at her feet. 'And I know I'm a bit chubby, but I *love* ballet and . . .' Again she paused and suddenly hid her face in the piece of paper.

'Don't spoil the paper,' her brother said, 'else you won't know what it says.'

7

Lucy Jane took the paper from her face. Her mother stopped making tea and went over to give her a cuddle.

'Come on, Luce darling, why are you being so silly? You managed to win the dancing competition last year and you danced in *The Nutcracker* at Covent Garden. You've always managed to do what you want before, so why are you upset?'

Lucy Jane couldn't answer. Going to Russia and having ballet lessons with the great Russian ballet mistresses meant so much to her, she found it hard to be sensible. She had heard the Russian dancers were the best in the world. If she was going to be a ballet dancer she wanted to train with the teachers who could help her to be as good as the Russians.

'First things first,' her mother said, taking her hand. 'Let's have tea.'

'Yes, let's have tea,' her brother repeated, climbing on to his chair.

'And we'll talk about this whole thing when Daddy gets home,' her mother finished. Lucy Jane nodded and dried her eyes.

'In the meantime,' her mother said, 'let me see the leaflet and I can find out about this special trip.' Lucy Jane immediately perked up.

'Yes, let's read it together, Mummy,' Lucy Jane suggested.

'*After* tea,' Mrs Tadworth said firmly, and she started to serve tea for her daughter and son.

That evening, when Mr Tadworth had returned from his work at the television studios, he read all about the Hirkov Ballet School. When he put the paper down he looked rather serious.

'It'll cost rather a lot of money, Lucy,' he said finally. 'And I'm worried that you'll be dancing and studying all through the summer holidays and won't get any holiday, and also . . .'

'I don't mind,' Lucy Jane interrupted. 'I did that last summer when I entered the dancing competition at the Albert Hall.'

'I know,' her father said slowly, 'but are you advanced enough? Maybe you won't be chosen. Grade IV? Sounds pretty high to me.'

'I'm getting better all the time, I've passed Grade IV and I'm practising for Grade V already,' Lucy Jane answered brightly.

'Mmm,' was all her father said. He was wondering if it was wise that Lucy Jane should miss seeing her grandmother in Scotland again this holiday and also, if she was chosen to go

9

to Russia, how would they cope with the expense of it all?

'If it's too expensive I could work,' Lucy Jane said eagerly.

'You may have to,' her father replied with a smile. 'Yes, help with the housework!' and he laughed. 'But I tell you what we'll do,' he said quietly. 'I'll talk to Mummy, then we'll talk to your teacher, and if she thinks you should go we'll see what can be done.'

Lucy Jane was content that at least some progress had been made. She knew there wasn't any point in pestering her father any more. 'I'll do my homework then my practice, and hope that my teacher thinks it's a brilliant idea for me to go,' she said as she went out. 'Because I do,' she added, peeping back into the room. She smiled cheekily at her father and disappeared.

Later that evening as Mr and Mrs Tadworth relaxed in their cosy sitting room, the first thing they discussed was Lucy Jane.

'It would be a wonderful experience for her,' Mrs Tadworth started. 'And it would finally give her a chance to know if ballet is what she really wants to do. She's nearly twelve and should start training seriously if she wants to be a dancer. Since the television film, she hasn't shown any real interest in acting.' She paused. 'But nearly two months at a Russian ballet school would be very hard work. And I know the Russian children are wonderful dancers,' she concluded.

Mr Tadworth didn't answer straight away. Although he had given up smoking he still chewed on the end of his unlit pipe when he was thinking. 'The problem is,' he said finally, 'it's so dammed expensive – eight hundred pounds. It's a lot of money.'

'I think it's quite reasonable for seven weeks,' Lucy Jane's mother replied. 'We're both working now, and I'm sure my mother will help.'

Mr Tadworth looked at her and said, changing the subject, 'I must get this work done tonight,' and he picked up the papers on his lap. He had to draw a lot of designs before going to the television studio the following day. So with a shrug he went to his study, leaving his wife to worry about her daughter's ballet plans on her own.

Upstairs Lucy Jane lay awake hoping her parents would agree to let her go. What Lucy Jane did not know was that persuading her parents to let her go was only one of the obstacles that lay in the way of making the dream come true.

At the end of the ballet class the following week after all the girls had done their *révérence* and curtsied beautifully, Miss Sonia, their teacher, clapped her hands and announced brightly: 'I need to know which ten boys and girls intend to audition for the Russian ballet school summer course.'

Lucy Jane's hand immediately shot up and she shouted, 'Me, Miss Sonia,' very loudly.

Miss Sonia looked at Lucy Jane and remarked, 'Yes, I thought you'd want to go, Lucy Jane, though I'm not at all sure if it's right for you at the moment. Do you really want to be a dancer?'

'I do,' Lucy Jane replied firmly. Miss Sonia looked doubtful, she could see that Lucy Jane had great potential, but was concerned that she didn't seem really serious about ballet.

'If only she remembered that I have danced at Covent Garden and won a dancing competition at the Albert Hall,' Lucy Jane thought, 'she would know that I am serious.'

Annette, who was the best dancer in the class, was standing near Miss Sonia, and told her, 'I'd like to audition too.' She did a little *pirouette*. Her light, slim body was perfectly proportioned and looked beautiful, no matter what step she performed.

'Yes, I'm glad you want to audition, Annette – you'll have no problems,' Miss Sonia said approvingly. Annette looked pleased.

'What about me?' Tom asked quickly, his dark curly hair and large bright eyes glowing at the idea.

'And me?' Johnny added, shaking his shock of red hair. His bold freckled face belied his rather shy character.

'Yes, all four boys should try,' Miss Sonia said, smiling.

'She always likes the boys best,' Marie, Lucy Jane's new friend, whispered out of the side of her mouth.

Marie was half French and her mother had been a dancer. Marie had dark brown eyes, with a pretty olive skin. Her fragile looks and fiery nature were quite a contrast to Lucy Jane's round face and bubbly personality. Marie's long dark hair was always shining and well brushed, and although she was cheeky, she looked as though butter would not melt in her mouth.

'Did you say something, Marie?' the teacher asked quickly.

'*Non. Non*,' Marie murmured in her very slight French accent. 'But I'd like to audition too,' she added wide-eyed, and then suddenly burst out laughing.

'What are you laughing about?' Miss Sonia asked.

'Don't know,' Marie replied, still giggling.

'She doesn't know anything, she's French, how can she?' Diana butted in, raising her hand to catch the teacher's attention.

Lucy Jane gave Diana a cross look but decided not to say anything.

'Let me have a go, too, Miss Sonia,' Diana continued eagerly. 'I'd like to go to Russia.'

Miss Sonia nodded to Diana, then looked at the class, and made her speech. 'The audition for those who have passed their Grade IV will be within four weeks. Those who have not passed Grade IV will have to wait until the end of term for me to decide. This is very serious, I want children who will really work and take advantage of this wonderful opportunity. It is a tremendous chance for any young dancer to train in Russia and I want my girls to be with the best and become the best.'

'End of term!' Tom exclaimed. 'That's another five weeks. My mum won't let me go if I don't decide TODAY.'

Everyone laughed and Lucy Jane wanted to applaud Tom's outburst, but she thought better of it and stood silently.

'There will also be a physical examination,' Miss Sonia continued. 'A doctor from the Royal Academy of Dance is coming to see which children have the correct hips and feet, the right potential to take the strain of serious ballet training in Russia.'

Miss Sonia looked at the children in turn. Suddenly all the girls and boys started to point their feet, stretch their backs and lift their legs into *arabesques*, testing their bodies, asking themselves if they would pass the physical examination.

There were only fifteen children in the class, but Miss Sonia already had her favourites. Lucy Jane was worried that, as she wasn't one of them, she might not be allowed to go to Russia. Luckily for her, at least four of the pupils in the class didn't really enjoy ballet so Lucy Jane was confident that they wouldn't want to spend their summer holidays studying ballet. Nevertheless, she was concerned that as she was plumper than the other children she wouldn't be considered classical ballet material.

Suddenly Miss Sonia clapped her hands again. 'Now, children, to give you some idea of the importance of physique and the physical examination, please watch Annette who has, to my mind, the perfect body for ballet. Look at her *extension!*' She asked Annette to do a *grand battement* to show how high and how easily her leg moved from the floor to above her head. 'Perfect, you see every line of the body is right. Every limb in the right position.'

Lucy Jane thought Annette looked rather smug. The height of Annette's leg annoyed Lucy Jane. She knew she couldn't kick so high. So she turned to Marie, whose *entrechats* were the best in the class, and said, 'What about your jumps, they're wonderful.'

Marie nodded, knowing her *élévation* was really good. Then whispered, 'And what about your back bends, Lucy Jane?'

'Mmm,' Lucy Jane agreed.

Both girls clung on to those positive thoughts as they wistfully watched Annette's perfect *arabesque*. Her leg stretched well above her head, her arms perfectly in place and not a wobble to be seen. In her heart Lucy Jane was a little envious, but she did not give up easily. She had overcome obstacles before. Why should it be any different this time?

Yes, she thought to herself, I'll practise more, eat less

sweets so I won't look chubby, and somehow or other I'll go to the Russian ballet school with the rest of them. This way I'll know if I really want to be a ballet dancer. Dreams are one thing, but to experience the day-to-day struggle for perfection will be the real test.

She was jolted back to reality by Miss Sonia's voice announcing, 'And one more thing, children. The school will be sponsoring the most promising pupil so that he or she can go to Russia, or one free place could be divided so four can go at less cost. Keep that in mind, children.'

Lucy Jane's eyes widened. Sponsored! If only she could be one of the children to share this sponsorship. Going to Russia had suddenly turned into a series of obstacles. Was she up to Grade V standard? Could she pass the audition? Would she get through the physical examination? Would her parents let her go or be able to afford it? Now Lucy Jane was determined to go to Russia and train with the Russian ballet dancers, she wasn't going to let anything stop her from fulfilling her dream.

2

Swan Lake

After the class the girls chattered as they changed out of their black leotards and pink tights. Next door the boys could be heard shouting and laughing in their changing room. But Lucy Jane and Marie were uncharacteristically silent. They were thinking about the Russian ballet school.

When Lucy Jane and Marie had changed and were outside the school waiting for their mothers, Lucy Jane turned to Marie and announced, 'I'll show that silly old cross patch, rag bag, pickle-faced, long-nailed ballet teacher Sonia Thingamybob that I can dance as well as Annette or anyone else!'

'Even if you do weigh more,' Marie added.

'Yes,' Lucy Jane had to agree. 'But what's five pounds when you want to dance? Mummy says I'll lose it as soon as I grow a little more, and if I eat properly, and,' the two girls said together, '*don't* eat so many crisps and sweets.'

'Yes,' Lucy Jane agreed, 'the doctor says I'd be exactly right for my size and age if I hadn't started eating sweets.' She looked at Marie and smiled mischievously. 'So let's have a jelly baby,' she giggled, and pulled a crumpled bag of sweets from her cardigan pocket and offered one to her friend. But in her heart of hearts she knew this had to be the last bag of sweets she ate.

17

In the car on the way home, Lucy Jane hoped her mother would want to talk about the Russian ballet school, but as she didn't mention it Lucy Jane asked politely, 'Did you have a nice day at work today, Mummy?'

Her mother paused for a moment, and replied, 'You know I only work three days a week, Luce, and today is not one of them. But yes, thank you, I had a good day.'

Lucy Jane's mother worked as a doctor at the local clinic, but on Tuesdays and Thursdays she always collected her daughter from ballet class after taking Jeremy to his swimming class.

Lucy Jane longed to mention the Russian ballet school, but suddenly her mother said, 'On Saturday afternoon I'm taking you to see the Northern Ballet in London. They have a wonderful production of *Swan Lake*. It is really original and I think it would be good for you to see.'

'Oh, I'd love to. You know how I've always wanted to see it.'

'Your aunt Sarah isn't working at the wardrobe at Covent Garden while the Royal Ballet are abroad, and she's with the Northern Ballet so you can see her too.'

Lucy Jane seized her chance: 'Can we ask her what she thinks of me going to Russia?'

'A good idea,' her mother agreed.

On Saturday morning Lucy neatly brushed her hair up into a little bun, to make herself look like a ballerina. She put on the dark green check dress, which Granny had bought her. Lucy Jane and her mother had an early lunch and set off to the theatre, leaving Jeremy with his father. It was lovely to have Mummy to herself for once.

Despite bad traffic and trouble parking the car, they arrived at the theatre in plenty of time. They were shown to plush red seats in the stalls. Suddenly the house lights dimmed, and the conductor walked into the orchestra pit. He wore a black dinner jacket and black bow tie. Everyone clapped as he bowed in a spotlight. Then he turned towards the orchestra, tapped his baton on the music stand and the musicians started to play. For Lucy Jane it was thrilling sitting in the dark, hearing the beautiful music sail over her head. Slowly the curtain rose and Lucy Jane gasped when she saw the beautiful scenery of a grey misty lake. Suddenly about twenty girls dressed as swans danced on to the stage, which was covered in mist. As they moved they really looked as though they were floating. They looked so beautiful, really like swans and Lucy Jane was surprised to see that they didn't look like photographs she had seen in which the dancers had their hair in buns and white feathers over their ears. These dancers had long dark hair flowing down their backs and instead of *tutus* they wore ragged white-feathered dresses, which fluttered and floated as they danced. Their eyes were made up with broad dark patches to look like the black markings swans have around their eyes above their beaks. When the dancers moved Lucy Jane could really believe they were swans. She turned to her mother excitedly and whispered, 'I want to look like that, dance like them.' Her mother smiled.

Then the young man who was Prince Siegfried, beautiful and full of fun, danced on to the stage. He and his comrades jumped and somersaulted in a wonderful tumbling act. Then a man dressed up as a mother bear came charging in on roller skates. He spun around all over the place deliberately knocking over the young dancer soldiers. Lucy Jane laughed so loudly that her mother had to hush her up.

When the ballet was over, and Prince Siegfried and the swan Odette had floated away together, Lucy Jane stood up and cheered loudly, almost crying with delight, clapping and jumping up and down. She turned and hugged her mother, she was so happy. It had been such a wonderful afternoon.

She didn't say anything, just squeezed her mummy, and Mrs Tadworth knew that giving her this treat was the best thing she could have done.

Lucy Jane and her mother went round to the stage door to see if they could see Aunt Sarah. As they waited at the stage doorkeeper's little lodge, Lucy Jane's heart started to beat with excitement.

'Miss Sarah won't be a moment,' the man said from behind the glass window. Lucy Jane thought he looked rather old, and although he smiled a lot, he could not take his eyes off the television he had in the corner of his cubby-hole.

Suddenly a voice from behind her screamed, 'Lucy Jane!' Lucy Jane turned round and there was Aunt Sarah, her arms outstretched and smiling a warm welcome.

Lucy Jane rushed over and flung her arms round her cuddly waist. Her aunt gave her a big squeeze and then greeted her mother.

'Want to come backstage?' she asked as she took Lucy Jane's hand.

'Yes, please.' Lucy Jane nodded excitedly. Her aunt Sarah was always laughing and in a good mood, and had been so kind when she had stayed with her while her mother was in hospital when Jeremy was born. It was during that holiday that Lucy Jane had met Tatiana Marova, the Russian ballerina, who was starring in *The Nutcracker*.*

'Remembering *The Nutcracker*?' her aunt enquired. Lucy Jane nodded again, she was gazing in wonder at dancers still in costume, who chattered and laughed as they rushed by.

'Come to the wardrobe and have tea,' her aunt said.

'Could we just look backstage first, please?' Lucy Jane pleaded.

'Have you got time?' Sarah asked her sister-in-law.

'Yes,' Lucy Jane's mother replied. 'It's wonderful when children really love something, isn't it?' she remarked to

*See *Lucy Jane at the Ballet*

Sarah as they walked along the corridor to the stage.

When they arrived in the wings Lucy Jane felt a surge of happiness at being so close to the stage again, and she closed her eyes with joy. She remembered being an understudy in *The Nutcracker* and having to dance when Alice sprained her ankle. She felt a little wistful and wondered if she would ever dance on stage again. She felt a longing for the excitement of performing. The magic, the smell of the theatre, the music, and the joy of dancing in public was all she wanted at this moment.

They stood for a minute in the huge dark space looking at the big round lights strung along steel bars overhead. The roof was so far away that, above the lights, rows and rows of painted backdrops hung like curtains ready to be lowered to be part of the scenery. The stage was almost completely dark, the footlights were off and the big iron fire curtain was being lowered to cut off the auditorium and orchestra pit from the stage. There were a few lights at the side of the stage, which cast mysterious shadows on the boat, in which Prince Siegfried and his beloved swan Odette had sailed away at the end of the ballet.

Everything looked rather dusty and old, which Lucy Jane found strange as she had thought it looked so beautiful from the front. At one corner of the stage there was a pool of light and two of the dancers were practising. They were dressed in rehearsal clothes and looked so thin that Lucy Jane thought if she touched them they would snap. The first dancer said in a Russian accent, 'At the Hirkov Ballet School we always dance *this* way,' and she demonstrated a few steps for her friend.

The word 'Hirkov' made Lucy Jane very excited. She tugged her mother's sleeve, but as her mother was watching the dancers she didn't notice.

'Well,' the second dancer said when the first had finished her steps, 'Miss Sonia does it like this,' and the second dancer showed her friend another way of dancing the steps.

'Miss Sonia!' Lucy Jane's voice burst out from the darkness at the side of the stage. 'Miss Sonia teaches me,' Lucy Jane went on excitedly. The two dancers stopped and looked round to where Lucy Jane was standing.

'I didn't know anyone was here. Who are you?' the second dancer asked.

23

Lucy Jane let go of her aunt's hand and rushed over to the two dancers. 'I'm Lucy Jane, I go to Miss Sonia, and I want to go to the Hirkov Ballet School this summer.'

'Well, you'll need to be on your toes with Miss Sonia,' the dancer replied quickly. 'She has her favourites. She's taught me since I was your size.'

Lucy Jane asked anxiously, 'Were you her favourite? How do you become her favourite?'

'Do extra practice with Miss Sonia after class,' the dancer said. 'She likes the girls that really work, you know, dedicated and keen. She used to dance with the Ballet Royal until she hurt her back.'

'I am,' Lucy Jane replied, her voice was small. 'Very keen.'

As Lucy Jane stood watching them, the two dancers

wrapped old cardigans round their shoulders. 'I'll get something to eat, before the next show,' the first girl said to her friend. Then she added to Lucy Jane, 'The Hirkov School is good, difficult, but very good. Good luck,' and she put on her leg warmers and scuttled away into the dark. 'Yes, good luck,' said Miss Sonia's pupil.

As the two dancers went off for tea, Lucy Jane felt the afternoon couldn't have been a greater success. It seemed as if everything was pointing the way to Russia. As if she was destined to go and see if she could become a ballet dancer. As she left the theatre she felt more determined than ever to do everything in her power to be good enough to go to the Hirkov.

3

The Surprise

At the end of Lucy Jane's next ballet lesson, while the other children were changing, Lucy Jane rushed up to her teacher saying, 'I saw *Swan Lake* on Saturday. You used to teach one of the swans to dance.'

'Ah yes,' Miss Sonia said, a little taken aback. 'Now that must be Nina.' She paused. 'Yes, Nina, she's in *Swan Lake*,' she continued, 'a very good dancer. Very keen, dedicated.' She looked at Lucy Jane, piercingly, and repeated, 'Dedicated.'

Lucy Jane wasn't quite sure if this was a good or bad sign, but she continued in a small voice, 'I'd like to be dedicated. Could you help me?'

'How do you mean?' her teacher replied, pleased that Lucy Jane was showing so much interest. She took off her ballet shoes and put them neatly in a plastic bag.

'Well,' Lucy Jane continued slowly. 'Every night I practise at home, but maybe I'm not practising the right way. So please could you help me?'

Miss Sonia looked at her and was silent. Lucy Jane continued, 'Please can you practise with me at the end of the class, so I can go to Russia.' A lump formed in her throat, fearing Miss Sonia would say 'no'.

'I'm afraid I can't do that, I have another class in Soho at six o'clock,' Miss Sonia replied matter-of-factly. Lucy Jane's hopes sank. 'But,' Miss Sonia continued, 'come on Saturday mornings. You can join in at the back of the professionals' class, no need to pay, and I'll help you when the class is over,' and she hurried off to change, not leaving Lucy Jane the opportunity to ask any more questions.

'But where is the class?' Lucy Jane called, desperate not to miss her chance. Miss Sonia turned back and smiled. Suddenly she realised that this little pupil, who she knew had potential, but didn't know how to develop it, was showing the determination needed to become a dancer.

'I'll see you *here*,' her teacher said, smiling. 'See you here at ten o'clock in this studio next Saturday morning.'

Lucy Jane could hardly believe her ears. She rushed into the changing room to tell anyone who would listen to her good news. 'I'm going to have extra lessons with Miss Sonia,' Lucy Jane told Marie as she took off her tights.

'So am I,' Marie announced.

'With Miss Sonia?' Lucy Jane asked amazed.

'With my mother,' Marie answered smiling. 'You know, she was a dancer.'

'That's wonderful,' Lucy Jane said, genuinely pleased that both she and Marie had a better chance of going to Russia.

'And, *ma chère* Lucy,' Marie said over her shoulders, as she pushed her practice clothes into her little leather bag, 'I'm going to show you all the things my mother teaches me, as long as . . . you tell *me* all the new things you are taught by Miss Sonia.'

'Of course,' Lucy Jane replied happily. 'Now we'll both be doubly good.'

* * *

Once Lucy Jane had finally persuaded her mother to let her have the extra ballet lessons with Miss Sonia, Saturday couldn't come quickly enough. On Friday night she slept in fits and starts and on the Saturday morning she was so excited she couldn't finish her breakfast. She even forgot to make her bed. As her mother drove her to the lesson she felt sick with excitement and could hardly talk.

'You're very silent, Lucy,' her mother said.

'I'm worried I won't be able to keep up and I'll look silly with the big girls as I'm not good enough,' she said.

'Don't worry,' her mother replied kindly. 'You'll be fine.'

When Lucy Jane walked into the studio most of the girls had already changed and were warming up in front of the mirror. Some of the girls were at the *barre* stretching and doing their *pliés*.

Lucy Jane wished her mother hadn't already left, as she was terrified and wanted to go home. As she crept between the dancers to the changing room Miss Sonia called, 'Lucy Jane, change quickly and come and stand at the *barre* behind Nina, and you can copy her.'

One pupil was standing with her leg resting on the *barre*, and stretching over so her head touched her knee. It was Nina! Lucy Jane couldn't believe it was her at first.

Butterflies buzzed in Lucy Jane's stomach and she rushed to change. She was so excited she put her tights on back to front twice and had to change them. Even her hair kept falling down and wouldn't go into a bun. By the time she was ready for the class she was really flustered. As she arrived at the *barre* a friendly arm suddenly went round her shoulders and Nina looked down at her saying, 'You're the lucky one to be invited into this advanced class. But if you watch me and do as Sonia says, you'll be fine.' Then she added, 'Ask me anything you need to know at the end of the class.' Nina pulled up her tights a little more and held on to the *barre*, her shoulders back, knees straight and feet in first position ready to start.

As Lucy Jane stood behind Nina doing her *pliés* and *grands battements* she felt extremely grown-up.

'Shoulders back,' Miss Sonia said, tapping Lucy Jane on the shoulder. Then she touched the leg Lucy Jane was standing on and said, 'Knees straight, pull up your knees and thighs more!'

Lucy Jane immediately did as she was told, never taking her eyes off Nina. 'Excellent,' Miss Sonia said, pleased that Lucy Jane responded so well to correction. 'This advanced work is good for you and I'm confident you'll succeed.' Then she walked on to the girl next to her.

Lucy Jane agreed, it was good for her, but very hard and in the second half of the class, when they moved into the centre, Lucy Jane was grateful that she had Nina to copy; and even more grateful to have someone to hide behind.

When the class was nearly over Miss Sonia said, 'Now, *grands jetés*,' and all the girls walked to the corner to do their *grands jetés* across the room.

Lucy Jane was praying she wouldn't have to dance on her own, but Miss Sonia insisted that she did. So she mustered up all her courage to dance her *jetés* alone across the room. To her embarrassment she made a terrible mess, and nearly fell over. But it made her more determined to do better the second time. Luckily for Lucy Jane her second jump was much better and when Miss Sonia said, 'Not bad, Lucy,' Lucy Jane was really pleased.

At the end of the class Lucy Jane waited quietly in the corner, exhausted and extremely hot. She was rather dizzy from trying to keep up with the advanced students, and practising so many new steps. Miss Sonia remarked as they were finishing, 'You really are a much more promising dancer than I thought.' This made Lucy Jane really happy. Then Miss Sonia said goodbye to all the girls, and suddenly, without even looking at Lucy Jane, Miss Sonia asked, 'Did you bring a snack to eat before we practise?'

'Yes,' Lucy Jane answered.

'What?' Miss Sonia replied.

'Some chocolate biscuits.'

'Right,' her dancing teacher said sternly. 'This is where we start.'

Lucy Jane looked at her, rather worried.

'To dance you must eat the right food, plenty of food, but it must be the right food. Junk food and chocolates won't make you strong, they'll make you fat. And when you're too heavy it's more difficult to dance, to jump or to look good in classical ballet.'

During this lecture Lucy Jane was feeling more worried with every word.

'What should I eat?' Lucy Jane asked bravely.

'Well, normal things like fruit – an orange. Bananas are excellent, or even a little milk or fruit juice. But these sweets I keep seeing you eat are useless for everyone, empty calories.'

Lucy Jane hung her head and was silent.

'I've got a wholewheat bread and honey sandwich or a banana in my bag,' Miss Sonia said in a gentler tone. 'Take your pick.' Lucy was learning that Miss Sonia was kind underneath the stern exterior. The ballet teacher opened up a paper bag and offered it to Lucy Jane who tentatively took the banana. 'Now eat that slowly, wrap up and keep your limbs warm. Rest for five minutes and then we'll do a little work on your footwork, *développés* and *adagio* steps. Going to the Ladies. Back in a few minutes,' she called as she walked to the door.

Lucy Jane went to the dressing room to put on her cardigan and leg warmers, then she returned to the studio and sat in the corner and slowly ate her banana. Soon her teacher returned with her hair brushed, fresh lipstick, and a broad smile. Lucy Jane immediately rose, ready to start her first practice with Miss Sonia. She knew this was her big chance to train to become good enough to go to Russia.

Miss Sonia made Lucy Jane do each exercise over and over again. 'Concentrate on your feet, keep those toes pointed. More. Again.' Lucy Jane didn't want to show she found it hard, but by the end her body ached all over from forcing her muscles, pushing her limbs to the limit.

Luckily each practice session became easier and Lucy Jane eventually began to feel that she was really improving.

'See how you've built up your strength, Lucy?' Miss Sonia said one Saturday. 'See how you've improved? Your turnout is much better and now when I see you dance I believe you are in control of your body and will become a dancer.'

Lucy Jane made so much improvement with the extra Saturday classes and practice sessions that, at ballet class a few weeks later, Miss Sonia clapped her hands at the end of the *barre* exercises and said, 'I would just like to show you what I think is the perfect line of head, hands, body and legs from the *développé* into an *arabesque*.' The girls shuffled around, expecting Annette to be called forward. When, to everyone's amazement, Lucy Jane was asked to demonstrate Marie squealed, '*Oh, mon Dieu!* Lucy Jane, it's you!'

Lucy Jane herself was taken aback, but walked steadily to take her place in the centre of the room. She hoped the pianist would accompany her as she always found it easier to dance when there was music.

But there was no music and Lucy Jane had to manage without. Nevertheless, she confidently lifted her leg to the side and turned into an *arabesque*. The line of her head, hand and leg were just as they should be. Her knees and thighs were well pulled up, her stomach strong and pulled in, her foot well pointed, her hand beautiful with no thumbs sticking out, *and* she didn't wobble.

'Very nice, Lucy,' Miss Sonia said quietly. She put her hand lightly on Lucy Jane's shoulder, saying, 'I can see now that you are really dedicated. You've made great progress *and*,' she added meaningfully, looking Lucy Jane straight in the eye, 'I notice you look a little trimmer. Not so many sweets, I imagine?' Then she winked at Lucy Jane so that none of the class could see. Lucy Jane was really encouraged by Miss Sonia's praise, and she went back to her place, delighted with the results of her hard work. Marie smiled and even Annette turned and said, 'Well done,' which really surprised Lucy Jane.

Pretending to be disappointed Marie grumbled, 'She never mentioned how much better my positions are.'

'No,' Lucy Jane whispered, comforting her. 'But I've noticed how much better you are.'

'Stop talking, girls,' Miss Sonia said, annoyed at the chatter. 'No time to mess about, next week there's the audition, and this week there's the physical examinations. In the next twelve days everything should be decided about who's going to Russia.'

A buzz of excitement and fear went round the pupils. Then suddenly a rather thin woman, wearing a long yellow chiffon scarf, crept into the room. None of the pupils had seen her before, and she crept over to Miss Sonia and whispered, 'Sorry, I'm late, dear, I'll watch some of the class, then I'll examine the children.' Lucy Jane looked at Marie, and Tom and David, who had also heard, opened their eyes wide and said, 'Examine!'

Miss Sonia looked worried. 'Liz, I had no idea you were coming today,' she said. 'I thought it was the end of the week,' and she turned back to the class, rather flustered.

The thin woman then went to sit on the edge of a chair by the piano, trying to pretend she wasn't there.

Miss Sonia clapped her hands and said sharply, 'Girls, come forward and do *grand battement, grand battement, grand battement, plié*, and *change*.' She used her hands as though they were legs to demonstrate what she wanted, determined to carry on with the class as though the stranger wasn't there. The four tallest girls moved forward and stretched their arms out into second position. Tom, David and Richard suddenly started pushing each other about and stupidly trying to distract the girls who were dancing.

Miss Sonia said angrily, 'Wait at the side of the room.'

The four girls continued their *grands battements*, trying not to notice the boys.

But everyone was very aware of the examiner perched on the edge of her chair as she peered at each child as they danced, making notes on a sheet of paper. When eventually the class was nearly over she rose and whispered to Sonia. Miss Sonia nodded and said, 'Children, go and stand at the *barre* while Elizabeth Cobb and I examine you.'

The children obeyed, mystified as to what was to happen. Then Miss Sonia and Miss Cobb walked slowly along the line, looking at each child and commenting quietly as they went.

34

Finally, Miss Sonia announced, 'This is Miss Elizabeth Cobb from the Royal Academy of Dance and she is going to measure your height, look at your turnout from the hips and your instep, knees, and so on.' The children looked bemused. 'So just do whatever exercises Miss Cobb asks of you. She will then decide which child has the correct body for classical ballet. You need to have feet that really point. Straight legs that lift easily. If you have tight hips, a curved back, hunched shoulders or knock-knees, you do not have the ideal body for classical ballet.'

While they waited at the *barre* Miss Cobb walked over to Annette and measured her height with a tape measure, and asked her age. She then made Annette point her feet and show her instep and lie on the floor so Miss Cobb could see how easily her legs moved in her hip sockets. Finally she moved Annette's legs back and forth to see how far they could go, and how easily she could turn out from the hip.

Tom, who was rather bored, decided to keep pointing his foot and showing off his high instep long before Miss Cobb had even reached him. But Miss Cobb took no notice and continued to mark down the details of Annette's instep, the height of her kick, and how well her feet and knees turned out. Then Annette was asked to bend backwards while holding on to the *barre*, and then forwards and touch her toes. Tom thought all these exercises extremely silly and said, 'Knees bend – 9 out of 10, high kicks – 3, lie on the floor leg lift – 7.' Miss Sonia was furious. 'This physical examination is extremely important,' she said. 'We must know which of you have bodies that can take the strain of the intensive ballet training in Russia.'

Lucy Jane went pale. She turned to Marie, looking very worried, and whispered, 'Suppose when I do my *pliés* my knees don't go over my toes enough. Suppose when I'm on the floor my hips aren't right, they're too tight.'

35

'My little friend, you are so silly!' Marie replied smiling at Lucy Jane. 'Many girls are no good for these things, but they still dance and go on the stage. Ballet is just ballet, it's not everything,' and she shrugged her shoulders as though it didn't matter to her if she passed the physical exam or not.

But to Lucy Jane it was everything. She wanted to go to Russia; she wanted to learn classical ballet; she wanted to dance on the stage again; and at this minute she wanted, more than anything in the world, to pass her 'physical'.

As Miss Cobb came nearer to her, Lucy Jane kept telling herself that if she didn't pass it didn't matter. But she knew in

her heart that if this happened she would be very disappointed. The problem was that she didn't really know what Miss Cobb was looking for, and as Miss Cobb hadn't indicated which girls or boys had passed, Lucy Jane felt even more helpless as she stood waiting for her turn. Her hands became so sticky with anxiety they could hardly hold on to the *barre*. She had to wipe them on her leotard. Suddenly Miss Cobb was talking to her, 'Now you show me your instep, dear.'

Lucy Jane immediately pointed her foot. Miss Cobb commented, 'At least no cycle.' Lucy Jane was relieved, as she knew a cycle foot was when the foot pointed inwards instead of out.

When Lucy Jane finished Miss Cobb's exercises, the effort of keeping her back straight, and holding her tummy in, made her hold her breath so long she thought she was going to burst. She felt pleased she had done everything as well as she could. As her mother always said, 'This is all you can ask of yourself.'

'Next,' Miss Cobb called, looking at Marie.

After the last pupil had been examined, an unnatural silence fell over the class and the children stood motionless, waiting to hear the results.

Elizabeth Cobb and Miss Sonia stood in the far corner quietly discussing the results on the sheets of paper. They nodded their heads and mumbled, the earnest expression never leaving their faces.

As the children began to get restless, Lucy Jane began biting her nails, a silly habit she had started the previous holiday. Marie touched her wrist and chuckled, 'If they do not choose us, Lucy – it is because we are too good.' This made Lucy Jane giggle.

Suddenly Miss Cobb walked into the centre of the room, touching her yellow scarf as she went. The children moved to make way for her. Her face was long and serious. Lucy Jane became so anxious that she wanted to go to the lavatory. Suddenly she couldn't wait any longer, and though she wanted to hear the results she put up her hand and asked, 'Please may I be excused for a moment?'

Miss Sonia didn't look at all pleased, but agreed and Miss Cobb began. 'Well,' she said wearily as Lucy Jane slipped out of the room. 'As much as I want to say you are all perfect, I can't. So rather than tell you one by one, I would suggest you each come with a parent to see me at the end of next week's class.' The children were silent and Miss Cobb studied her papers. 'But would the following children come and see me individually today. Tom, Marie, David, Annette, Simone, and . . .' She was just about to say the next name, when the door squeaked open and Lucy Jane crept back into the room. 'And,' she continued, 'and Lucy Jane.' Lucy Jane looked concerned and rushed over to Marie.

'What's happening?' she whispered.

'Must go and see Miss Longface and hear the bad news.'

Lucy Jane's heart almost stopped.

The six children mentioned went meekly over to Miss Cobb and stood silently looking up at her. Miss Cobb looked back at them for a time not appearing to care whether she put them out of their misery or not. Eventually she said, 'Tom, David, Annette, Simone, Lucy Jane and Marie, you have the correct requirements for classical ballet. Miss Sonia and I would like you all to audition for the Russian ballet course. You are all very lucky children. You each have in different ways the ideal build for ballet. Good luck!' and she walked away without another word.

Lucy Jane was so relieved that she had passed the physical examination, and now she knew that it was only the audition standing between her and going to the Hirkov Ballet School. Or, at least, that is what she thought.

4

The Audition

'Mummy, Mummy,' Lucy Jane shrieked as she rushed into the house after Marie's mother, Madame Le Coeur, had delivered her home. 'I passed, I passed,' she shrieked again. Mrs Tadworth was delighted, but she had no idea what Lucy Jane had passed.

'I passed the physical exam and all I have to do now is pass the audition and I can go to Russia.'

'Not so fast,' her mother said. 'Daddy still hasn't agreed, we haven't asked Granny to help – so there's more than an audition to pass before going to Russia.'

Lucy Jane's heart sank. 'Well, I may get a scholarship or something, as they said one or four of us may be helped, if we are really good.'

Mrs Tadworth didn't hold much hope of Lucy Jane getting a scholarship to go to Russia, but she kept these thoughts to herself as she went on preparing supper.

'Oooh, spagaletti,' Jeremy said as he saw his mother put the spaghetti into the boiling water.

'Spaghetti, not spagaletti,' Lucy Jane corrected, rather annoyed at her mother's lack of enthusiasm. 'I'm not hungry,' Lucy Jane said grumpily.

Her mother didn't answer and started to make the tomato sauce. 'Lay the table, Lucy. And, Jeremy, please collect the napkins from the drawer.'

'How can I draw napkins – I haven't got a pencil,' Jeremy said. This made Lucy Jane laugh. She forgot her sulk and helped her brother get the napkins and lay the table.

Before Lucy Jane went to bed she decided to have one more try at persuading her mother and father to let her go to Russia.

'Now listen,' her father said impatiently, 'pass the audition first and then we'll think about it. But it's no good worrying about something that may never happen.'

Lucy Jane knew her father was right. But it still annoyed her that he thought it might never happen. It also annoyed her that he wouldn't just say 'yes' and be done with it. So she went to bed feeling very upset.

'Granny would say "yes", I know, if I asked her,' Lucy Jane mumbled as she went upstairs.

Mrs Tadworth didn't like to see her daughter worrying, so when she went upstairs to kiss her goodnight, she gave her an extra long hug and said, 'Lucy, be wise, don't pester Daddy. If you pass, and if we can afford it, we'll let you go. But you must learn to be patient, and not nag us every time you don't immediately get your own way. Let's not trouble Granny at the moment, we don't want to worry her.'

Lucy Jane knew she had been silly, but she wouldn't admit it to her mother. She just gave her a big squeeze and snuggled under the covers to go to sleep. Suddenly she sat up and announced brightly, 'I know. We could use some of the money I earned doing the television film.'* Her mother thought for a moment, then agreed it would be a good idea.

'Yes, that's very sensible,' she said. 'We can think about that when you pass, in the meantime go to sleep and get your strength.' Then she kissed Lucy Jane goodnight.

On Friday morning, the day of the audition, Lucy Jane rose extra early to practise and pack her ballet clothes. She had washed her tights the night before and put them in the airing cupboard to dry. She had also washed her hair ribbon and wound it round the hot pipes so it would dry smoothly and look as though it had been ironed. When she had packed, she went down to the kitchen, and took an orange to put in with her practice things.

After breakfast she rushed to put on her school blazer and waited anxiously by the front door, longing to set off for school.

The journey, the lessons, and lunch seemed to drag on interminably. Even the journey in the minibus from school to the ballet studio seemed longer than usual – so much so that Lucy Jane whispered to Marie, 'The driver must be lost this week. We're going all over the place, we're going to be late.'

'Rubbish,' Marie reassured her. 'Mr Jones is taking his usual route.'

Lucy Jane looked out of the bus window and dreamed of what it would be like to be in Russia. There would be the thrill

41

of having a classical ballet class twice a day, and a chance of really knowing what it would be like to be a dancer. She would enjoy the struggle for perfection, maybe even suffer. Suffer, after all, is what all great artists have to do for their art. Give up day-to-day pleasures, in order to have enough time to work and practise. Lucy Jane knew if she wanted to achieve great things she had to be prepared not only to work hard, but also to sacrifice little things she took for granted, like watching television, seeing her friends, and other things that took time she'd need for practising. Tatiana Marova was always practising, even backstage between the scenes when she was dancing *The Nutcracker*. If Lucy Jane was to be like her, she, too, would have to devote her whole life to dancing.

Suddenly the bus squeaked to a halt and Lucy Jane was jolted from her dreams and scrambled with the other children from the bus.

Annette, who was sitting at the front, climbed down first. Unlike Lucy Jane she looked relaxed, as though she was really looking forward to the audition. Marie, too, didn't seem in the least bit worried, and the boys at the back of the bus were so noisy, and cheerful, that Simone and Mrs Sampson, one of their form mistresses, had to try and silence them as they jumped from the bus, laughing and singing. No one but Lucy Jane seemed nervous.

Lucy Jane changed as quickly as she could. She was anxious to be ready before the others, so she could warm up in front of the mirror, like the students at the Saturday morning class. So she quickly peeled her orange, took one piece, and hurried into the studio and started to practise at the *barre*.

Little by little the boys and girls drifted into the studio, some rather silent, others relaxed and some giggling and doing silly things to hide their nerves.

When Miss Sonia entered the room, the children went

quiet. Then to their surprise a rather severe-looking woman, with black hair scraped back into a bun and wearing a red dress, black stockings and little high-heeled fur booties, followed her. The boys and girls all looked at each other, wondering who she was.

'This is Isabelle Whyte, the ballerina. She has studied at the Hirkov Ballet School and has also taught there. She has come to help me audition you.'

'We thought only you were auditioning us,' Tom said.

'Just go to the *barre*, children. We'll do an ordinary *barre*. Then Isabelle will ask you to do a special series of steps, your *enchaînements*, once you come to the centre.'

Miss Sonia looked at the pianist, Miss Moon, and nodded her head. Miss Moon played a loud dramatic chord on the piano and the children rushed into position. 'So away we go,' Miss Sonia said, smiling. 'Don't let me down, as I know Miss Whyte is expecting great things of you.' And the class began.

Marie stood behind Lucy Jane at the *barre* and Lucy Jane was behind Tom, who was behind Simone, who was behind Annette, who was at the head.

Lucy Jane did each exercise hardly knowing what she was doing. The fear of failing the audition had turned her into a numb block, and now all she wanted in the world was for it to be over.

As the children turned from one side to the other and changed the hand holding the *barre*, Miss Sonia gave them a quick wink and Lucy Jane suddenly felt in control of her body and ready to do her best to impress Isabelle Whyte.

Miss Sonia looked quite pleased as she watched her pupils. They were all dancing as well as they could, even the boys looked serious and were not fooling around.

As the audition progressed Lucy Jane became more and more confident. She suddenly felt she could dance her very best. The joy of the music seemed to fill every muscle of her body and she danced her *enchaînements* as if she had been doing them for years.

Miss Whyte nodded to Sonia, 'Very musical children in this group,' and she looked at the four girls dancing in the front row, Annette, Marie, Lucy Jane and Simone.

At the end of the audition the children were asked to improvise a dance to a piece of Tchaikovsky's music. First they had to listen to the music, then in turn dance whatever steps the music made them feel they wanted to express. Lucy Jane had always loved improvising. She had done it so often at home. At the weekends, sometimes for hours on end, she would play tapes and make up dances to the music, dancing all around her tiny bedroom. But here she had plenty of space and was longing for her turn. Both Simone and Annette danced rather nervously, and only did the steps they had already done in the class. Marie's dance was full of flourish and fun. Lucy Jane watched her admiringly. She was dying

44

to dance next but the boys all had to dance, by which time she was longing to go to the lavatory and had to leave the room as Tom leaped around the studio.

When she returned, Miss Sonia said, 'You next, Lucy.'

Now Lucy Jane wished she had danced first and had it all over with. But as soon as Miss Moon played the first chord Lucy Jane sailed into her improvised solo. And a great solo it was. Her shining presence, combined with many of the new steps she had learnt in the Saturday morning class, and some she had made up as she went along, made her dance very special. At the end she spun round the studio like a top, glided into a fall on the floor like a snake, and ended up rolled over on her tummy. The children burst into spontaneous applause at her originality. Lucy Jane knew she had danced with all the passion and love she felt for ballet.

When the clapping died down there was a long silence. No one spoke, no one moved, not even Miss Moon. Miss Whyte and Miss Sonia walked to the far end of the room, chatting quietly and nodding as they went. All Miss Sonia said to the pupils was, 'Please go and change, children.'

The boys and girls scuttled into the changing rooms to get ready to go home. When they returned to the studio Miss Sonia and Miss Whyte were still talking at the far end of the studio, their heads bent in discussion.

Tom and David suddenly shouted, 'Here we are – tarrra!!'

Miss Sonia looked round.

'Well, do we go?' he asked smiling, not looking at all nervous about the results.

Miss Whyte looked at Miss Sonia and said, 'May I speak, Sonia?'

Miss Sonia nodded.

'There are only two children in this group who may not go to Russia.' Lucy Jane and Marie looked concerned.

'There are three children who will have some help with

their expenses and qualify for a scholarship.'

Annette, Marie and Lucy Jane exchanged hopeful glances. And then Miss Whyte said, 'But I do not wish to give you the final results now. You will receive a letter tomorrow morning informing you if you have passed.'

'Tomorrow morning,' Tom said, appalled at the thought of waiting another eighteen hours.

'Yes, tomorrow,' Miss Whyte confirmed.

'Well, that puts paid to a good night's sleep!' Tom said.

The children said goodbye to Miss Whyte and quietly left the room, disappointed that after all they still did not know the result.

5

The Result

The next morning the postman arrived late, although Lucy Jane had hoped he would arrive early. She had been awake and waiting for him most of the night. She was finishing her breakfast when she heard the plop of the post through the letter box. She immediately rushed to pick the letters up and give them to her mother, her heart thumping.

'Open them! Please open them quickly,' Lucy Jane pleaded.

Mrs Tadworth looked at the letters in turn and put the bills to one side on the table.

'Is it about me?' Lucy Jane asked anxiously as her mother read one of the letters.

'No, this is from the Planning Office about our application for permission to extend the kitchen,' her mother replied.

'What's in the next letter?' Lucy Jane said, anxiously hopping from foot to foot.

'This is . . . Oh, yes, Lucy, this one is about you,' her mother said excitedly. Lucy Jane held her breath.

'Well, I never!' Mrs Tadworth exclaimed, and sat down.

'Well, I never what?' Lucy Jane squeaked.

'Listen to this,' her mother continued. 'We would like to offer Lucy Jane a grant of £300 towards her expenses.'

'Expenses, yes, but does it say I can go?' Lucy Jane insisted. 'Have I passed? Can I go to Russia?'

Mrs Tadworth read the letter again and gave her daughter a squeeze. 'You *can* go to Russia.'

Lucy Jane let out a yelp of happiness. 'Can I see it?' Lucy Jane asked, anxious to see the result with her own eyes.

Mrs Tadworth passed the letter to her. Lucy Jane nervously put on her glasses and then slowly put the letter on to the table. She looked up at her mother with tears in her eyes. 'I can't believe it, I *can* go to Russia,' she said, her whole face now shining with happiness.

'Yes,' her mother replied, 'and they are giving you £300 towards your expenses, which is a wonderful thing, as Daddy felt £800 was rather a lot.'

Lucy Jane suddenly went quiet, worried that her problems still were not over.

'But now,' her mother continued, 'with the money you earned last summer on television and our contribution, you will be setting off to the Russian ballet school in a few weeks' time.'

Lucy Jane could hardly believe the wonderful news. She prayed her father wouldn't stop her, but she would have to wait until he came home from work to find out.

That evening, to Lucy Jane's delight, her father came home early. He didn't seem at all tired and when Lucy Jane bounced up to him waving the letter from the ballet school, he smiled happily and gave her a hug. 'What's new?' he asked, as he looked at his daughter's excited face.

'We've had a letter about Russia,' she said breathlessly, 'I've passed and I've got a sort of scholarship – £300!!'

Mr Tadworth looked surprised and took the letter from his daughter. 'Come, let's sit down,' he said, anxious not to conduct the whole discussion about Russia in the hall.

So Lucy Jane followed her father into the sitting room.

'Ooh,' he exclaimed loudly after he had finished the letter. 'This is most impressive, Lucy.'

'Does that mean that you will let me go?' Lucy Jane begged her father, desperate for a final 'yes' after all her weeks of work and worry.

'If you use your pocket money to buy your new ballet shoes,' he said, 'you can go. And if Granny lets us use a little of your Christmas and birthday money towards the trip,' he continued. 'And Mummy and I give up any treats for a while, and you use some of your television money I'm sure we can get enough money together for you to go,' her father replied laughing.

Lucy Jane was so happy to hear this she immediately hugged her father. 'And what is Jeremy going to give up to help me go?' Lucy Jane asked. 'That's what I'd like to know,' she finished with a twinkle.

Her father smiled and pinched her cheek, kissed the end of her nose and sent her off to do her homework.

★　★　★

Now that Lucy Jane's visit to the Hirkov Ballet School was finally settled she felt her feet would never touch the ground again. She would no longer resent doing extra jobs around the house. But the weeks leading up to the trip to Russia became the most tense Lucy Jane had ever experienced. Although the school organised the air tickets and the visas – the certificates the girls needed to go to Russia – they also sent each pupil an endless list of the required ballet clothes and belongings. Lucy Jane was secretly filled with self-doubts about her dancing. She knew the Russian children were extremely good dancers, far more hard-working and dedicated than many English children. Most of the children at Lucy Jane's ballet school were serious about ballet and many of them thought they wanted to be ballet dancers. They imagined dancing was just wearing pretty dresses and receiving bouquets of flowers in the spotlight at the end of the performance. They didn't think of the hours of practice, aching muscles and hard work. As Lucy Jane and her friends only did two or three ballet classes a week, the high standard of the Russian children, who danced every day, would be a big challenge to them. Lucy Jane was worried but she kept her fears to herself and practised even harder, as Miss Sonia said this was the only way to achieve the same standard as the Russian children.

When the day of departure arrived Lucy Jane looked pale and sick. She had been on a plane before, she had even flown alone to see her granny in Scotland. But she had never been abroad to stay in another country without her parents, a country where they didn't speak the same language, or eat the same food.

As she stood in the big Departure Hall at Gatwick Airport, tears rolled down her cheeks. She gave her mother and father and brother Jeremy a squashy goodbye kiss.

'Got your pocket money and Russian dictionary?' her mother asked. She was trying very hard to cheer her daughter up.

'Yes,' Lucy Jane mumbled quietly.

Her father squeezed her hand and stuffed a little package into her pocket. 'This is for you to open on the plane,' he said kindly. Lucy Jane looked up and smiled. Then Jeremy handed her his pencil and said, 'This is for you to write to me on the plane.'

Lucy Jane laughed and took the pencil, gave them each another kiss and went off to join the rest of the children standing with Mrs Sampson, the mistress from their school who was going with them. As they waited patiently to go through Passport Control, Lucy Jane waved to her parents and blew them a last kiss, before she entered another world.

Once on the plane Lucy Jane quickly forgot her sadness. She looked forward to the adventure that awaited her. She sat between Marie and Tom.

'What's that sticking out of your pocket?' Tom asked, seeing the package peeping out of Lucy Jane's cardigan.

'Oh, that's a present from my daddy,' she said, quickly removing the package and opening it. Inside there was a little bear wearing a ballet dress and glasses and a tiny message round the neck. Lucy Jane read the words: 'To our little ballerina, thinking of you all the time, love from Mummy, Daddy and Jeremy – X'

Lucy Jane kissed the bear. She felt happy and warm inside. She knew that while she was away the bear would be her mascot and link her to home. After a while they were served food on little trays, and Mrs Sampson walked up and down the aisle between the seats, chatting to the children and checking that they were behaving well. Then they saw a funny film on a little screen in the middle of the plane and they wore earphones like a Walkman to listen to the sound.

The film was about a large naughty dog. The plane journey passed more quickly than they had expected. By the time the film was over the plane was about to land. They all packed up their bits and pieces ready to take their first steps on Russian soil.

Lucy Jane and Marie felt really excited as they waited for their luggage to arrive. Lucy Jane took out her Russian/English dictionary to look up the word 'please' only to discover it was written in letters she couldn't understand or pronounce. She felt bad that she hadn't asked about these words. The children were supposed to have had half an hour of Russian a week before leaving, but unfortunately the woman who was going to teach them fell ill, so now they had to make do with a phrase book and a dictionary.

Once their bags arrived they were hustled into a minibus to go to the ballet school The journey through the streets was not at all as Lucy Jane had imagined. She had thought she would see magnificent buildings with gold onion-domed roofs and coloured tiles like pictures of Moscow on television. But the bus didn't go anywhere near Moscow and the buildings were plain and grey, the food shops had empty windows and there was none of the glitter and brightness of the big stores in London. Instead, the large windows had a few plain dresses standing on old-fashioned stiff models, with no frills or decorations.

Suddenly the minibus screeched to a halt outside a very dilapidated building with cracked plaster, peeling paint, and one or two broken windows. The girls and boys looked at the crumbling building in dismay as they collected their bags to descend. Lucy Jane said, 'Jumping cactus, this looks like a prison.'

'It is,' Tom said. 'Only worse!'

No sooner had the girls clambered down from the minibus than a broad-beamed lady bursting out of a floral blouse, and wearing a shiny tight black skirt that didn't cover her knees, spoke to the girls in an English almost impossible to understand.

'Children, come with me.' The children, still carrying their cases and rucksacks and plastic bags, followed the galleon-like creature into the building and straight into a large empty studio. The children had hardly arrived in the room before Madame Krotchenova, the principal of the school, a thin woman all in black, clapped her hands and began, 'First I want to tell you, to be dancer you have to suffer. You have to be prepared to suffer.'

Lucy Jane was listening intently, not wanting to miss a word she said. She had to learn the secret of how to become a great ballerina.

'I will say no more tonight,' the principal finished abruptly. 'Please go to your rooms, but to dance you must believe the pretty dress are not good enough, if legs are no good and the

heart is in the wrong place, nothing is good.' She stopped. 'Tomorrow the first class is at nine o'clock. Be prepared to suffer!' and away she sailed with the large lady, leaving behind the English pupils standing motionless, mouths open and amazed. It was not the welcome they had expected, but it was a taste of things to come.

6

The New Life

Lucy Jane squeezed Marie's hand excitedly as they walked down the drab corridor looking for their room. Although there was no carpet on the floor, or any pictures on the walls, and the paint was peeling, she felt a tingle of excitement.

'I'm not going to be homesick,' Lucy Jane whispered as she carried her suitcase and clutched the tiny bear her mother and father had given her.

'Well, if you want to be a dancer you've got to be "prepared to suffer",' Marie giggled, imitating the principal.

Lucy Jane agreed. They arrived at the door marked Marie Le Coeur and Lucy Jane Tadworth.

'This must be us,' Lucy Jane said excitedly, and she opened the door and peered in.

The room was drab, much plainer than they had imagined. There were just two beds with a small rough wooden table between them and six, large rusty hooks on the walls on which to hang their clothes. Lucy Jane thought of her room at home, so comfortable and pretty with the matching curtains and bed covers, and the stencilled flowers round the walls, that she and her mother had painted in the Christmas holidays.

'I suppose the rooms are plain so the dancers don't think about anything else but ballet,' Lucy Jane observed.

'Yes, this room would make any dancer long to get away and practise,' Marie agreed as she put her suitcase down and plonked herself on the bed. It creaked and sounded as if it was going to break. Lucy Jane looked at the ceiling. There was a crack like a large spider's web. She smiled to herself, too tired to be disappointed. Their room was not important. What was important was that she was lucky enough to have been chosen to study at one of the great Russian ballet schools. This was her dream, and she was going to make the most of it.

The next morning the two girls woke early, eager to start the day. Lucy Jane followed the other children into the huge airy studio for her first ballet class. Suddenly she was gripped with fear. She clutched her ballet shoes and walked through the vast old studio, wondering if she would be good enough to stay the course. She knew she wasn't as good as Annette. Her *élévation* was not as high as Marie's, who could jump at least five inches off the ground when she did her *changement* and *entrechats*. But what really worried her was what the Russian children would be like.

The studio was much larger than she expected and rather cold, as all the windows were open and there was a cool draught blowing, despite the warm weather outside. There were enormous, old mirrors round the walls and in the corner there was a baby grand piano with a thin man with long floppy hair practising arpeggios. By the piano was a rickety old chair and a watering can. Lucy Jane joined the other children in the cloakroom. When she had put on her leotard and pink tights, she immediately went to the *barre*, doing up the belt round her waist as she went. Tom tried to pinch her as she passed, and although Lucy Jane was not really cross she was annoyed that he could be so silly on their first day.

The ballet mistress, Madame Nureova, who was rather fat, immediately tapped her thin bamboo cane on the wooden floorboards when she saw Tom being silly, and said, '*Niet, niet, niet*. No. No. No. Please, no nonsense.'

Luckily, Lucy Jane knew now that '*Niet*' meant 'No' and '*Da*' was 'Yes'.

The ballet mistress then took the little watering can and passed it to Annette, indicating to her to sprinkle the water over the floor. The wooden floor was duly sprinkled with water so the students wouldn't slip. Madame Nureova, who was much older than Lucy Jane had expected, looked extremely fierce, and shouted in a big voice to Tom and David as they went to the *barre*. 'Close the window.'

The boys immediately did as they were told and rushed back to their places. 'Back straight,' she said and tapped the children between the shoulder blades with her thin cane.

It was really painful and made Lucy Jane's eyes smart. It was not the only time the children were to feel Madame Nureova's cane as she used it a great deal. Lucy Jane wondered if it was because she found it difficult to express herself in English.

At the end of the first class the children were utterly exhausted. The class was extremely challenging, and they found it hard to keep up, especially as they had arrived only the day before, and still had not got their bearings. After the class they changed and a new teacher, whom they had seen briefly the day before, appeared. She was Madame Dragonova, who seemed to be in charge of the day-to-day running of the course and ordered them to go to the dining room for lunch at twelve o'clock.

Madame Dragonova was older than the other ballet mistresses and was always cross. But she felt that this was her role, to discipline the children and make sure they didn't complain. She had a slight limp and carried an old walking stick, which had three little bells on it, so everyone knew when she was coming. Her clothes were rather loose and long and always black. Despite the fact it was summer, she looked dressed for the winter.

The dining room was huge, gloomy and uninviting, and the smell of cabbage and stale vegetables wafted around, making them feel sick. As they sat at long wooden tables on broken wooden chairs, with a bowl of soup and bread in front of each place Lucy Jane, who was really hungry, suddenly felt quite faint.

David turned to Tom and said cheerily, 'Oliver Twist had a better life than this.'

Lucy Jane agreed. 'See how the Russian ballerinas struggle and suffer to be as wonderful as they are.'

'Is it worth it?' Tom replied turning up his nose at the first taste of soup. Then he spat it back into the spoon.

'Behave yourself,' Annette said sternly.

Their first lunch at the ballet school was a disaster as far as the children's taste buds were concerned, but it was also an eye-opener as to how people lived in Russia. Poor food and not much of it. This was not what the English children were used to, but it was what they would have to accept.

That evening when the children had finished their second class of the day, they were exhausted and were unusually quiet. The school building was so large they often got lost. Few people spoke English and they still had not managed to talk to any of the Russian girls and boys. This was not surprising, as the English children couldn't speak a word of Russian, except *'niet'* or *'da'*. But even if they had been able to talk, the Russian children were so dedicated and serious, they did not dare to speak to the English children. They did not dare do anything that would spoil their chances of graduating from the Hirkov Ballet School or being chosen to go to New York to dance in a demonstration of Russian ballet. The English children felt a little sad they might never get to know their Russian counterparts.

After several days of hard classes and Russian lessons, Mrs Sampson, who was very motherly and sweet, took the children on their first outing. For a treat she decided on a tea shop for tea and cakes. The children had been starved of fruit and sweet things since they arrived. There was a cry of joy, and the children got ready so quickly that Mrs Sampson almost forgot her handbag with her *roubles* to pay for the tea.

On the way to the tea shop, Lucy Jane was terribly shocked when she saw a lot of children in the street, huddled in doorways and at the side of the road. They were dressed in rags and looked as if nobody cared for them. 'Look,' Lucy Jane whispered to Marie. 'Why are there so many street urchins?

Marie didn't answer and hurried Lucy Jane past the begging children anxious to catch up with Mrs Sampson. 'I expect they're orphans and there's no orphanage,' she said finally, thinking more of her tea than the ragged children.

At that moment they arrived at the tea rooms. There was a long queue outside, and Lucy Jane and Marie were amazed that they had to queue for nearly two hours to get in. It was, as usual, another hot day. Lucy Jane had always imagined Russia would be freezing with snow, even in the summer, but it was so hot they had to fan themselves constantly. The heat, of course, was ideal for dancing, as their bodies were always warm and the children never complained that their legs were too stiff to dance, as often happened in the winter at home.

As they stood in the queue waiting to get into the tea shop, they could see in through the big glass window. The café was very simple with plastic covers on the tables, and to the children's disappointment, there was not a large selection of cakes. Lucy Jane thought wistfully of how many rich things there were to eat at home.

When at last they arrived inside the shop and it was their turn to order, there were only just enough cakes left to go round. The lady serving had a large, smiling well-polished face. When she heard the children speak English, she could not stop laughing. '*Keks*,' Lucy Jane said in her best Russian at the counter. She pointed to a large sugar bun and held up her *roubles* to pay. The laughing lady handed her the cake wrapped in a piece of paper. Lucy Jane had rather hoped they would sit down and be served cups of hot chocolate and have several cakes. But Mrs Sampson said they had no time for that as the queue had taken so long. 'Can't be easy to be Russian,' Lucy Jane said to Marie as they left the shop, looking at her sticky bun.

'Can't be easy to be a cake, or *keks*,' Marie replied as she took the first bite of hers. As the children walked home Mrs Sampson allowed them to eat their cakes in the street. Annette looked disapproving and said, 'Shouldn't really do that in the street, it's bad manners.'

Suddenly three little children, the smallest looked no more than three, rushed out of a doorway and tried to snatch a piece of cake. Then lots more children, all extremely thin and dirty, appeared and begged for cake from the other children. Soon masses of children swarmed round them, begging and snatching the cakes from their hands.

'They must be starving,' Tom said, as his cake was taken from him.

'So am I,' David said, stuffing the last morsel of cake into his mouth, before the begging children could snatch that too.

'Come on,' Mrs Sampson said, as she hurried her group away as quickly as she could. 'I should have warned you,' she said rather anxiously. 'There are lots of children who live on the streets here, as their parents can't afford to feed them and keep them at home.'

'Why?' Lucy Jane asked, worried.

'Because people have more children than they want,' Mrs Sampson replied.

'Why?' Lucy Jane asked again.

'Because they don't know how not to have children.'

The experience of seeing so many hungry children was so disturbing that when that evening, Lucy Jane looked at her bowl of soup and the thick chunk of bread, she did not dare complain.

'*Dégoutant!*' Marie said. 'No wonder the Russian ballet girls are so thin. They get nothing to eat.'

'They need to be thin to dance,' Lucy Jane replied. 'I wish I was thin.'

'Yes,' Marie agreed, 'but not half-starved. You have to eat to grow properly and feed your brain. Now we know what we read in the English papers is true. The Russian girls aren't getting any proper food and now neither are we.'

'Well, there's nothing else, so we'll have to eat it,' Lucy Jane said.

'Better than the roast badger we had the other day,' Tom said.

'It wasn't badger – it was leather pretending to be meat,' David replied.

Tom stood up and made a face, and Simone and Annette, who were next to him, pulled him down as they saw Madame Draganova enter the room.

'Who speak not enough food?' she said sternly, looking at the children in turn. 'Who no like food?' she asked again. The children were silent. Then Tom piped up, 'Why don't we eat with the Russian children?' Everyone went quiet. 'Because they get better food than we do,' he said, almost to himself.

'All children have food same,' Madame Dragonova said crossly.

'Same rubbish!' Tom said, not caring whether he got into trouble or not.

Madame Dragonova walked over to Tom and held him by the ear. 'When you great dancer you choose food. But small boy eat food on table and no complain as you no great dancer.' She let go of his ear.

'I'll never be a great dancer at this rate, as I'm HUNGRY.'

By the looks of the children's faces they all wanted to agree but they dared not. 'Madame Dragonova,' Annette explained politely, 'Tom is right, we are hungry.'

'And our parents can't send us food as it takes eight weeks to arrive,' Lucy Jane continued.

'And we miss fruit and sweets and tomatoes,' Marie finished, looking Madame Dragonova straight in the eye.

'Russian children,' Madame Dragonova said firmly, 'are great dancers by sixteen and Russian children eat same food.' She tapped the floor with her stick and the bells jangled as she walked from the room. The children finished their bread and soup in silence, hating Madame Dragonova and her tingling stick more than the food itself.

7

'My little star'

As the weeks passed the children became used to their new life and were no longer complaining that everything was not the same as it was in England. They had to work really hard. There were mime and National and character dancing and ballet classes.

At the second class on Saturday Lucy Jane had a wonderful surprise. They were all standing at the *barre* ready to begin when a familiar soft sweet voice said, 'I take the class today, Mrs Sampson. Madame Nureova and Madame Sedova are away, and also I have a bad neck, I am not performing at the theatre tonight.'

As there were often different teachers Mrs Sampson didn't find this unusual, and she replied warmly, 'Oh, what a great honour that you should teach the children. They are so lucky and privileged to have you. I saw you dance in London. I would love to stay and watch the class, if I may?'

'Welcome,' the new teacher replied, and she nodded to the pianist to strike a chord on the piano for the class to begin, and Yuri, the pianist, flicked his hair back and began to play. As soon as the children heard the music they immediately stood very straight, feet and arms in first position ready to start.

Lucy Jane was sure she had heard the voice of the new teacher before, but she was not sure where. She did not dare turn round but she could feel the ballerina walk along the line, getting closer as she corrected the children at the *barre*. Suddenly she stopped by Lucy Jane and watched her do her *battements tendus*. After a moment she said, 'Pull knees up more, point foot more.'

Lucy Jane still did not turn round, but now she was certain she had met the ballerina before.

When at last she saw the woman's face she could hardly believe her eyes. It was Tatiana Marova, the ballerina from Covent Garden who had starred in *The Nutcracker*. She had been so kind to her. Lucy Jane was about to open her mouth to speak, when the ballerina moved away so she did not have a chance, and Lucy Jane continued to do her *battements tendus* as best she could.

By the end of the class Lucy Jane was bursting with excitement. She was now positive it was the great Russian ballerina, Tatiana Marova. But she wondered whether Miss Marova would remember her. The amazing coincidence of meeting her again was a chance in a million. At the end of the class, after everyone had curtsied or bowed, Lucy Jane waited a moment then walked over to the ballerina, and said, 'Miss Marova, do you remember me? I was in *The Nutcracker*.'

Miss Marova was silent for a second, then suddenly let out a great 'oh' of delight. 'My little star,' she said, hugging Lucy Jane. 'My little star,' she repeated. 'How lovely to see you. You remember Miss Softpaws, my cat? She will also be happy you are here.' She looked at Lucy Jane a moment and said, 'I am very happy you want to be a dancer,' and she gave Lucy Jane another squeeze. Lucy Jane could hardly hold back the tears. Then the ballerina and the little girl stood holding hands a moment, looking at each other.

'You change or your legs get cold and stiff,' the ballerina

said, so Lucy Jane quickly went off to change.

As Lucy Jane took off her pink tights and black leotard in the changing room, Annette asked enviously, 'Do you know her?'

'Yes,' Lucy Jane replied, not wanting to boast or show off.

'How?' Simone asked, not believing Lucy Jane.

'I worked with her at Covent Garden,' Lucy Jane replied.

'Well,' Marie said, 'let's hope we get some special treatment at last.'

Lucy Jane, too, hoped people would be nicer, especially Madame Dragonova. She also hoped that Tatiana Marova would inspire them to dance even better.

Suddenly there was a knock at the door. The girls were still getting out of their leotards and rubbing their legs and arms down with a towel, when a voice said, 'Children, please come to the studio.'

The children quickly wrapped their towels round their necks, finished struggling into their cotton tracksuits, and rushed back into the studio. When they arrived, the boys were already there, and to the girls' amazement they had already changed and their hair was combed flat with water, and they were looking very hot.

Miss Marova waited until the children were silent. 'Today,' Miss Marova started, 'was a good surprise. English children work very well and the boys are strong.' The children looked pleased. 'I think we will make a video for Russian television of Russian and English children dancing together in the same show.' She paused. 'Yes?'

The children nodded happily.

'We start extra work on Monday. Rehearsals for two dances for the video.'

There was a buzz of excitement. The English children felt that at last they would get to know the Russian children. After a moment Annette was the first to speak. 'We would love to do a television show with the Russian dancers and . . .' she looked at Lucy Jane, hoping she, too, would say something. Lucy Jane took up her cue and added, 'We'd love it even better if you'd rehearse us for the show.'

All the children clapped at the idea of Miss Marova taking

the rehearsals. Miss Marova smiled. 'I am very happy,' she replied. Walking towards Lucy Jane she said, 'I met Lucy Jane when I danced in London. I am very happy to know you all, and be friends with many English future ballerinas and dancers.' The children clapped again. 'We will make a terrific show.'

The children all wanted to show their enthusiasm but they knew if they were too noisy that Madame Dragonova would arrive, with the bells on her stick ringing, so they just clapped quietly. But even so, Madame Dragonova appeared with her orders, 'Work – silence,' and left the room.

Miss Marova smiled kindly. 'Not to worry, she was always angry even when I was your age. Now she's older, she's even more angry.' The children nodded. 'But she has a very good heart.' The children weren't so sure about this but they were delighted that Miss Marova had taken them under her wing.

The arrival of Miss Marova created great excitement. That evening, as the children queued in the corridor for the only telephone they were allowed to use to ring their parents, Mrs Sampson said, 'You all seem full of beans and very happy tonight.'

'We are,' Lucy Jane replied, smiling. 'Miss Marova, our new teacher, said we can be in a television show with Russian children, and we start rehearsing on Monday.'

Mrs Sampson looked really pleased. Miss Marova had brought a positive goal to the course and the hard work and long days would seem even more worthwhile.

'Now you will have something very special to show your parents,' Mrs Sampson said as Simone angrily clacked down the telephone. She was again unable to make a reverse charge call to her mother.

'And it may be shown in England,' Lucy Jane continued hopefully.

Mrs Sampson suddenly changed the subject. 'By the way,' she said, 'I have a small request from Madame Dragonova. She has had complaints from the ballet mistresses.' The children all looked at her. 'She is rather annoyed that firstly you are not always wearing clean tights, and secondly . . .'

She could not finish as Marie butted in quickly. 'Can't get into the bathroom to wash them.'

'One moment,' Mrs Sampson said firmly. 'And secondly,' she repeated, 'she thinks that many of you are not taking proper care of your ballet shoes.'

'What do you mean?' Simone was annoyed as her clothes were always beautifully looked after.

'Well, ribbons are not properly sewn on, or washed, shoes are not folded with ribbons wrapped round when they are put away, *pointe* shoes are not correctly darned. In general,' she finished, 'there is an air of slovenliness which is not good enough.'

The children all shuffled about and made grumbling noises, but no one disagreed as they knew it was true.

'Well, enough of that,' Mrs Sampson said brightly. 'It's been a good day. You have a great opportunity. So off to bed,' and she led the way to the bedrooms with the children following her.

When the lights were out Lucy Jane whispered to Marie, 'Seeing Miss Marova reminds me of home. I feel really homesick.' She was almost crying.

'Oh, Lucy,' Marie said, not prepared for this outburst and jumped from her bed and knelt by Lucy Jane's head.

Lucy Jane hid her head in the pillow. She was also feeling rather silly that she was so upset. 'I miss everything,' Lucy Jane said. 'It wouldn't be so bad if we had letters. But nobody has had a letter, no food parcels, nothing.'

'It's because the post is so slow,' Marie reassured her.

'Yes, I know,' Lucy Jane sniffed. 'But at least we're going

to do a proper show with the Russian children, and it's going to be on television,' Lucy Jane said, drying her eyes.

'Mmm,' Marie agreed as she jumped back into bed and snuggled under the covers. 'But I don't think we'll get much of a chance, as the Russian girls are so good.'

'All the more reason to be better,' Lucy Jane replied.

They could hear the sound of Madame Dragonova's stick and bells being dragged along all the dormitory doors as she called, 'Sleep time. Tomorrow, half after eight, ballet class big studio. Eat half after seven, studio eight, start half after eight.'

The repeated chant and banging stick died away as she continued down the corridor.

Lucy Jane waited a moment, then whispered, 'I haven't spent any of my pocket money yet, have you?'

'No, neither have I. Nothing to buy,' Marie replied quietly.

'We'll have to buy something to take home to our parents,' Lucy Jane went on as softly as she could, terrified that Madame Dragonova might hear her.

'We've got another three weeks to worry about that,' Marie said. She was not interested in present buying.

'Yes, and we've only three weeks to worry about learning the new dances,' Lucy Jane reminded her.

'*Oui*,' Marie said, and sighed. '*Oh, mes jambes*,' she grumbled, rubbing her legs and turning over to go to sleep.

'Are your legs aching too?' Lucy Jane asked, wanting to go on talking. 'Mine are as well. Every morning I wake up aching all over – it must be all this practising.'

'*Non*,' Marie replied. 'It's no proper food and old age!'

This made Lucy Jane burst out laughing so loudly that Madame Dragonova came storming back down the corridor and barged into their room.

'Who speak?' she said fiercely.

Lucy Jane and Marie were silent.

'Who speak?' she repeated, turning on the light and looking at the girls. Both girls huddled under the covers and pretended to be asleep. Madame Dragonova flicked the bedcovers back with her stick and said again, 'Which girl speak?'

Like twins, a terrified Lucy Jane and Marie both sat bolt upright and replied in one voice, 'Me.'

The girls looked so funny that the corners of Madame Dragonova's mouth broke into a smile. This surprised the girls so much that for a moment they forgot they were frightened of her and jumped out of bed and rushed over, 'Sorry, Madame,' they said together and gave her arm a little squeeze and looked up at her appealingly.

Madame Dragonova smiled and replied, 'No speak now, bed. Remember class,' and she left the room.

'I think she was crying,' Lucy Jane whispered.

'That's because everyone hates her and she thinks we don't,' Marie replied very quietly, anxious not to be caught again.

'Well, it's true, we don't,' said Lucy Jane firmly, putting her bear mascot on her pillow. 'At least, not any more.'

Marie wasn't quite sure if she agreed, but the two girls pulled up the covers and this time they did go to sleep.

The next morning after their eight-thirty ballet class Tatiana Marova said, 'Now from tomorrow every day there will be an extra class after lunch to rehearse for the video. You must work really hard.'

Lucy Jane was delighted at the thought of extra dancing instead of Russian lessons, although she was pleased she could now say a few Russian words.

To everyone's surprise Madame Dragonova then ushered in eight Russian girls and six Russian boys wearing practice clothes. They moved silently across the studio and stood

quietly in the corner. The English children watched them in awe, they looked so disciplined, so perfectly groomed as they stood straight-backed, their feet in first position and their hands by their sides. None of them spoke or moved. Like little statues they ignored the English children and looked adoringly at Tatiana Marova as she gracefully walked to the centre of the room, gently rubbing her neck, which was still sore.

'I introduce,' she paused and looked at the Russian children, then repeated in Russian, 'the Russian students to the English students.' She held out her hand to the Russian children and they walked over as a group to shake hands. The Russian children were noticeably thinner and the girls seemed smaller-boned and shorter for their age. The Russian boys were much bigger with large calves and developed thighs, and their muscles could be seen clearly beneath their tights.

'What huge legs,' Marie whispered.

'Shh,' said Lucy Jane, terrified they would be caught talking and be sent away.

'You all dance for the television together,' Miss Marova continued in Russian and then in English. All the children smiled at each other and acknowledged Miss Marova with a nod.

'You will rehearse together every day, and eat at the same place, same time. So now you can make friends.' She smiled at the students.

The children were delighted at the idea of eating together and shouted, 'Yippee! Hoorah,' so enthusiastically that Madame Dragonova immediately appeared, banging her stick, saying, 'Stop, stop.' There was silence except for the bells on Madame Dragonova's stick jingling as she walked away. When she had gone the children quietly left the room for their next class. Soon they would have their first meal together. They could get to know each other.

8

'Getting To Know You'

At their first meal together, the Russian children were already waiting in the dining room when the English children arrived. The moment they entered the room there was a chorus of 'Getting to Know You' all sung in Russian, except the first four lines.

> 'Getting to know you,
> Getting to know all about you,
> Getting to like you,
> Getting to hope you like me.'

When they had finished Lucy Jane, Marie and all the children burst into loud applause and rushed over to the Russian girls and boys, who took them by the hand and sat next to them at the table.

It was a lovely surprise and broke the ice perfectly. All through lunch the children tried to talk to each other in broken English or Russian. There was lot of laughing and sign language and even Madame Dragonova seemed pleased to see the children really trying to be friends.

Then came the first rehearsal together for the television video. As the children crowded into the huge studio, Miss

Marova, Madame Sedova, Madame Nureova, and even Madame Dragonova and Mrs Sampson, came into the room. Tatiana Marova once again spoke first in Russian, then in English. 'I want children in two groups,' she said. 'Each group will dance two dances. Learn the first dance this week, the second next week. The last week we rehearse all the dances. The solos I teach separately.'

There was a buzz of excitement as to who was going to be in which group, and who was to learn which dance. To Lucy Jane it was a dream come true. Great ballet mistresses teaching them new ballets to dance with the Russian children. And she was going to be on television again.

Annette, Marie and Simone hugged each other excitedly when Miss Marova announced her plans. Even Madame Dragonova seemed pleased as she looked at her piece of paper and divided the children into two groups. One group went to the green studio, the second stayed where they were. Miss Marova asked Madame Sedova and Madame Nureova to go with the children to the green studio, while she stayed with the group of Russian and English children, including Lucy Jane, in the great studio.

'Please sit, children, sit,' she said as she walked to the piano with a piece of music. She nodded to Madame Dragonova who left the room. 'Now we hear the music and afterwards we learn the dance.'

The children quietly sat waiting to hear the music. It was lively music, a Russian folk dance which made the children feel they wanted to dance the moment they heard its resounding chords and strong rhythm. When Yuri, the pianist, had finished playing Miss Marova said, 'We will hear this dance called *Gopak* again.' Then she called, 'Now, Tom and Vladimir, close the windows by the piano, Rudolf and David open the window by the door.'

The four boys immediately leapt up and did as they were

told. Then Yuri played the *Gopak* again, his long hair waving around as he pounded the piano. Miss Marova nodded her head and did little steps with her fingers, hands, and then feet. 'Now,' she said when the pianist had finished. 'Six boys here,' she pointed to one corner of the room, 'and six girls here,' pointing to the other side.

The children divided into two groups and Miss Marova started to teach them their Russian folk dance.

At the end of the rehearsal the children were so hot and tired, they almost collapsed. As they dried down their legs and arms, and wearily changed for supper, even the prospect of stewed leather and cabbage didn't seem to bother them, they were too exhausted to care. But they still made an effort to talk and get to know each other, and Russian and English dictionaries were on the table. They got along famously. It was a good start to the most important phase for the English children at the Hirkov Ballet School.

Two weeks before the performance, the children were practising every spare moment – in corridors, as they were waiting outside the bathroom, in the dining room, in the bedrooms. Not a moment was wasted, the practising was so intense that Madame Dragonova tried to stop it. Some of the children had Walkmans and had recorded the music for their dances so they could rehearse with the proper music. The Russian children did not have any gadgets like this, so the English children shared these luxuries with them.

'Please, no work more today,' Madame Dragonova said as she walked down the corridor filled with children practising, and music blaring. The children obeyed for five minutes, then as soon as she was out of sight they immediately started rehearsing again. Tom, David, Rudolf and Vladimir, who were now firm friends, thought that no more work was a terrific idea and repeated, 'No work more,' very loudly. But

no one took any notice and they continued to practise.

By the last week the rehearsing got to fever pitch. The English children were so anxious not to be outshone by the Russian dancers, who had been studying ballet for longer and were far better.

As the big day drew nearer the costume fittings and extra rehearsals filled every spare moment. The tension and excitement increased with each hour and many of the children complained of sleepless nights and not wanting to eat.

'Hardly surprising we don't eat, the food is rubbish,' Tom said rudely.

'*Oui*,' Marie agreed, 'we are very thin now.'

'Well, in my case,' Lucy Jane added, 'it's a good thing. Miss Sonia will be happy, I've no tummy,' and she tapped her stomach. 'If only the letters and food our parents sent us would arrive,' she sighed longingly.

'I know,' Marie said. 'My mother told me on the telephone that she had sent four boxes of raisins and some nuts weeks ago.'

'But the post is so slow,' Lucy Jane agreed gloomily.

'Why does it take eight weeks for a parcel or letter – where does it go?' Tom asked Vladimir who shook his head and shrugged his shoulders.

Vladimir was one of the best Russian dancers. He was always smiling and helpful, but he was worried that the English children seemed so upset about the food. Suddenly he announced, 'My mother make *keks*. I to school take. You eat.'

A great 'ohh' of delight went through the dining room and the English children serenaded Vladimir with 'Getting to Know You'.

When Mrs Sampson came into the dining room she was happy to see the Russian and English children being so friendly and that the preoccupation with English food and longing for letters was diminishing.

Lucy Jane and Marie became very friendly with Anna and Karina, two of the best students in the Hirkov school. Anna and Karina were dark-haired quiet girls, with lovely smiles and sparkling personalities when they danced. Like most of the Hirkov students they lived for ballet. They ate, slept, drank ballet. They had started dancing when they were three and had had a class every day, sometimes twice a day, since they were five. They had no other life and talked of nothing else. Dedication and hard work were all they knew. They had none of the distractions of the English children, such as sport, hobbies or television. But they never grumbled, never said something was too hard, or the hours too long. They just worked and danced and dreamt of being ballerinas.

As the Russian girls did not have personal stereos to play the rehearsal music Lucy Jane and Marie shared theirs with them. They also let Anna and Karina borrow their tape when they had finished rehearsing together, so they could practise. 'We must copy the way they dance as much as we can,' Lucy Jane remarked as they watched Karina and Anna that night.

'Yes,' Marie agreed. 'They dance beautifully and have fabulous technique. *Magnifique!*' and she blew a kiss to the air in a gesture of admiration.

The girls were, without doubt, the most beautiful young dancers that Lucy Jane and Marie had ever seen. But the Russian girls were much more temperamental than the

English children; they flared up easily if they were angry when they could not do a step properly, or made a mistake.

'*Niet, niet, niet,*' Anna said angrily to herself as she failed to finish her pirouettes facing front. 'I go mad. I mistake make again,' she sighed to Lucy Jane as she did not finish her *chaîne* turns properly.

'Everything you do looks wonderful to me,' Lucy Jane said truthfully.

'*C'est vrai,*' Marie agreed, imagining that if she spoke French it would be easier for the Russian girls to understand her.

The following morning, at rehearsal, Miss Marova said she was concerned about the children's health. 'Please take extra care before the recording,' she pleaded. She didn't want any of her dancers unable to perform because of injuries or strained muscles. 'Tonight, physiotherapists are coming to

see all the children,' she continued. 'All the children will have their legs and backs examined and have a massage.

'And,' Miss Marova said dramatically, 'tomorrow I shall take all of you to Moscow to see a ballet performance. Be ready at two o'clock.'

There was a gasp of excitement from the English children, especially Annette and Lucy Jane, who had been longing to go to the ballet ever since they had arrived. 'Tomorrow!' they repeated, beaming at Miss Marova.

'Yes, the ballet will inspire you before your television performance.' Miss Marova replied. 'We want great dancing from all of you, and in Moscow you will see great dancing.'

Simone was worried they would not have enough money to pay for the seats. By the time they had returned to their rooms she had managed to create such a feeling of panic that the children, especially Marie, were really upset.

'Tell me, how are we going to pay?' Simone fussed. 'The ballet is very expensive.'

When Mrs Sampson arrived to find out why the children were late for lunch, the discussion about the cost of the seats had risen to fever pitch.

'What's this? What's all this nonsense about money?' she asked, furious that although the children had a wonderful treat to look forward to, they were still grumbling.

'We're worried we won't have enough money to pay for the ballet seats,' Lucy Jane and Marie replied, looking up at Mrs Sampson with tragic faces.

'Now, children, be sensible,' Mrs Sampson began. 'You know Miss Marova wouldn't suggest going to the ballet if you couldn't afford it, and as it happens, theatre seats are very inexpensive in Russia.'

'How inexpensive?' Simone asked immediately.

'About twenty to thirty pence,' Mrs Sampson replied triumphantly.

'Twenty pence!' the children burst out. 'Twenty pence to go to the ballet!'

'Yes, concerts, theatre and ballet are subsidised by the government. They help to pay the cost of running the companies, so the seats don't have to be expensive,' Mrs Sampson concluded.

'That means everyone can afford to go,' Lucy Jane said pleased.

'Well, in principle that's the case. But as you must have noticed, many of the people here are extremely poor, so even twenty pence is too much to pay to go to the theatre.' Mrs Sampson looked at the children. 'Now hurry along to lunch. Don't forget, tonight you all have an appointment for physiotherapy. I'll meet you in the big studio at five, then we can work out in which order you go to see the four physiotherapists.'

At five o'clock the children went in their groups to the physiotherapists to have their legs and backs examined. Then they each had their legs massaged with oil while Mrs Sampson stood and took notes of any injuries before the children went back to their rooms. Those waiting to go to the physiotherapist went for yet another costume fitting.

'I love this costume for the *Gopak*,' Annette said, preening herself in the mirror. The huge coloured skirts with aprons and the white blouses and red bodices flattered all the girls and made them look very pretty. They also had red knee-length boots which came up to the frilly white petticoats under their skirts.

The boys had baggy black trousers tucked into their high red boots and floppy white blouses with round necks, fastened at the side. The large red sash round the waist made the costume look really dashing.

Each girl had two costumes, and for the second dance, the *Moon Ballet*, they wore all-in-one multi-coloured leotards

and tights, with huge chiffon butterfly wings dotted with sparkly sequins. Some girls had flowing tunics that were tied up over one shoulder leaving the other shoulder bare, instead of the wings. Both costumes were pretty and easy to dance in, which was important as the steps were classical and needed a great deal of control and technique.

Anna and Karina, who both did *pointe* work, had a solo each and a *pas de deux* with one of the boys, and for this they had the classic *tutu*. But Lucy Jane and Marie did not have a real solo, they just danced a few extra steps in the middle of the Russian dance with one of the boys. It was an 'almost solo', as Lucy Jane called it, enough to get excited about but not enough to worry about. Needless to say both Lucy Jane and Marie were so keen that they had learnt everybody else's solos, in case they had to perform them. This was unlikely, but nevertheless they were prepared.

9

Moscow

The next afternoon they were all ready at two o'clock to leave for Moscow and the ballet. The children hoped the bus would arrive in Moscow on time, so they could drive round the city and go to Red Square and see the Kremlin. As they stepped on to the coach they were each given a package of very dry uninviting-looking sandwiches, wrapped in rough paper.

'Tea from Sanivar in Moscow and ice cream at Gum shop,' Madame Dragonova, who was wearing a green scarf to brighten up her usual black, announced to the children as they took their sandwiches. At the word 'ice cream' all the children's faces lit up. Russian ice cream was famous for being the most delicious in the world.

Mrs Sampson, Madame Nureova and Madame Sedova also clambered on to the bus. Only Miss Marova was missing. But just as the bus was due to set off, she arrived, looking very glamorous in a white suit with a red silk rose on the lapel.

'Now we go!' she said happily as she sat down next to Madame Dragonova and the coach drove away. 'Now we go to a great ballet.'

The bus bumped its way through the countryside and drab towns with streets lined with building upon building of grey blocks of flats. There were not many trees in the streets and much of the countryside looked dry. Huge spaces stretched on either side of the road, massive areas of woodland and fields. Suddenly Madame Dragonova stood up and said, 'Now eat food. Ice cream and tea in Moscow.'

Vladimir immediately stood up after her and said, 'For you my mother give *keks*,' and he held up an enormous home-made cake.

'How lovely and kind,' Lucy Jane enthused. She knew how hard it must have been for Vladimir's mother to spare the eggs and flour.

'*Délicieux*,' Marie agreed, and both girls stood up and blew a kiss to Vladimir, who went very red and immediately sat down again.

When they reached Moscow the English children all gasped in amazement at the gold and white onion domes on top of the buildings, shining in the afternoon sun. No photos had prepared them for the astonishing sight. The streets were enormously wide, and when they arrived in a vast square the bus stopped and Madame Dragonova said, 'Walk in Red Square, see Kremlin, eat cake, ice cream, and in one hour and half, ballet.'

The children immediately got off the bus, they were very sticky and hot. They looked about them quite humbled by the size and unusual beauty of the impressive buildings. The dark blue domes with gold stars outlined across the skyline were like beautiful crowns.

'The big golden domes on top of the red brick buildings are much more wonderful than the pictures,' Lucy Jane said excitedly to Marie.

Karina and Anna were happy to see the English children so impressed by the beauty of their capital. After they had walked round the square they stopped at an old-fashioned tea room, where they had tea without milk from a *samovar*, which was a huge tea urn. They drank from tall glasses with metal handles. They ate Vladimir's mother's cake, which he cut with great care in order to divide it into twenty-six pieces.

After tea they set off to Gum's for ice cream. They had all been longing for the ice cream and they were not disappointed.

The next stop was the ballet. They passed the large fountain and stood in front of the Bolshoi Theatre.

The theatre had eight tall white columns at the entrance and as they went up the steps of the magnificent white building its size and beauty took the children's breath away.

Inside there were tier upon tier of seats and boxes all around the side, and branched gold electric candles lit the auditorium. It was like an amazing red and gold wedding cake rising up to the sky.

'We are going to see the Rivaska Ballet Company,' Miss Marova said. 'It is a really great company, it's my company.'

'As great as the Bolshoi?' Lucy Jane asked, surprised.

'Yes, now the Rivaska and the Kirov and other new companies are as great as the Bolshoi.'

Lucy Jane was quite taken aback. She had always thought the Bolshoi was best, and she was rather disappointed she was not going to see them.

When the lights went down and the curtain rose, all the children sat motionless and captivated at the magnificence of the production of *Spartacus*. It was a vibrant, exhilarating ballet, based on the story of how Spartacus freed the slaves. The children's eyes almost smarted with excitement at its energy and passion.

On the bus home Miss Marova said, 'Now you have seen how dancers give their whole soul to dance. I want your love for the dance to show when you dance on television.' The children heard and silently agreed. 'I want to see your heart in your work not just your bodies. I want to be proud of all of you.' She looked at each child in turn, her eyes seemed to smoulder. She was dazzling and so beautiful as she willed them to give a magnificent performance.

That night, as Lucy Jane lay in bed cuddling her bear mascot, she was so inspired by *Spartacus* and Miss Marova that she went through all the steps of her two dances in her head. She had to be sure that she knew every movement perfectly. She thought about *Spartacus* and how the principal dancer had jumped so high and shown such extraordinary strength. She thought of dozens of slaves filling the stage and dancing as though their lives depended on it, leaping with

every muscle taut and landing so quietly, like a cat. Lucy Jane thought of her *pas de chat* and understood the importance of landing quietly, toes first like a cat, and why the step was called *pas de chat*. When finally they stood with their swords raised, holding Spartacus above their heads on the steel blades, it was a sight to behold. The exhilarating experience would live in Lucy Jane's memory for years to come. *Swan Lake* had been so graceful and moving, the gentle beauty of the dancing such a contrast to the energy of *Spartacus*.

Now she understood the passion and energy Miss Marova wanted when they danced the *Gopak*. To dance as though they really knew the steps, not as if they had just learnt them.

After such a wonderful evening Lucy Jane felt she really was prepared to sacrifice everything to be a dancer. Lucy Jane was prepared to suffer like Madame Krotchenova had told them their first day. Lucy Jane now knew what she wanted most in the world, to dance.

The next morning there was a great commotion. 'Simone, Sonia and Karina are all ill,' Marie cried as she rushed down the corridor looking for Lucy Jane.

'Ill?' Lucy Jane replied alarmed.

'Yes, they've been really sick and Madame Dragonova says they can't dance in the show tomorrow.'

'But they all have solos,' Lucy Jane answered anxiously.

'Yes, I know,' Marie continued, 'and someone has got to dance them.'

'All of them?' Lucy Jane asked, alarmed.

'Yes, except Karina. Madame Dragonova says she will film hers another day. I wonder who will dance in their place?'

'I don't know who knows their solos,' Lucy Jane replied.

At that moment Miss Marova came hurrying along the

corridor. 'All the girls must go to the big studio immediately,' she called.

Lucy Jane and Marie called the other children to join them and they rushed off to the large studio. When all the girls, English and Russian, had arrived Miss Marova looked at them with a grave face and said, 'I have bad news. Three girls are not well and cannot dance for the television tomorrow. Karina will film her dance when she is better, but two childrens must dance for Simone and Sonia.'

The girls all looked at each other in a panic.

'We will audition now for replacements. If you want to dance a solo please put up your hands,' Miss Marova finished.

Everyone put up their hands except Marie and Lucy Jane.

'Don't you want to dance a solo?' Miss Marova asked them.

'We're already dancing a little bit on our own,' Lucy Jane said quietly, imagining that this would exclude her. But she really longed to have the chance to dance the extra solo.

'So do Annette, Anna and many other girls,' Miss Marova said. 'So why not dance more? If you want to be in a ballet company, you must be greedy for the spotlight – not shy or too modest. Please put up your hands.'

Lucy Jane and Marie put up their hands and immediately Miss Marova said, 'Good. Now all the girls will audition for the small solo of Simone and the big solo of Sonia.'

Lucy Jane suddenly felt sick but she squeezed Marie's hand and whispered, 'This is our chance.'

Miss Marova tapped the piano with the toe of her *pointe* shoe and said, 'All girls change and audition in ten minutes.' Then she sat down by the piano, opened a thermos of iced tea and had a drink.

When all the girls were back in the studio she asked, 'Which girls already know the solo?' Lucy Jane, Marie, Annette, Tanya, Natasha, and Luka put up their hands. Miss Marova was disappointed as she looked at the others. 'Girls who are not interested enough to know all the solo dances can go.' The four girls who didn't know the solos went shame-faced back to the changing room. 'Now listen to the music again, then all dance the solo together, then I will watch each girl dance, one by one.'

The girls danced the solos a little nervously. Then Miss Marova clapped her hands and called, 'Annette, you first.'

Annette walked to the centre of the room and started her solo. She danced extremely well and made only one mistake towards the end, but Miss Marova looked pleased and asked her when she had finished, 'Do you fit into Sonia's costume?' Annette replied that she didn't know and went to wait by the *barre* at the side of the studio.

Luka danced next and she too danced extremely well.

Miss Marova looked pleased and asked her the same question. Luka replied 'yes' and went to wait next to Annette.

Then it was Marie's turn, and once again Miss Marova looked pleased as she asked her if Sonia's costume would fit her. Now only Lucy Jane, Natasha and Tanya were left to dance. But Tanya suddenly burst into tears and said she was too nervous to audition.

Lucy Jane was so upset to see Tanya crying that she followed her into the cloakroom to comfort her. Miss Marova looked on in dismay. 'Dance – not time to cry. To dance you must be courageous, determined; no time or place for a weak heart. Natasha, dance, please.'

When Lucy Jane returned Natasha was just finishing and Miss Marova said, 'Lucy Jane, you dance now, please.'

Lucy Jane didn't have time to be nervous, or wonder if Miss Marova would just mention the costume again. To Lucy Jane's disappointment she did. But then Miss Marova paused and looked at all the girls slowly. 'Please, Lucy Jane, Marie, dance again. Then Natasha and Annette.'

All four girls walked forward and Lucy Jane and Marie

danced Sonia's solo together. They danced it so prettily and
with such unity and charm that Miss Marova suddenly said,
'Stop, stop,' even before they had finished. 'I like this dance
with two girls together, very nice. Now, Annette, Natasha,
please, you dance.'

Annette and Natasha didn't dance so well together. When
they had finished Miss Marova sat down looking very pen-
sive and she cradled her chin in her hand, her body bent
forward from the waist.

'What do you think, Yuri?' she said to the pianist. Yuri
pointed to Lucy Jane. Lucy Jane went red and Miss Marova
walked over to her. 'Yuri agrees with me,' she said. 'You
dance very well, my heart has a happy feeling when I watch
you dance. I want you and Marie to dance Sonia's solo
together. It will be a *pas de deux!*' and she smiled at them.

Then she looked at Annette and Natasha. 'I think Annette will dance the first half and Natasha will dance the second half of Simone's solo as you girls do not dance so well together, but you do dance well.'

All four girls looked very pleased, especially Lucy Jane; nothing could be nicer than the two friends dancing together.

Now Lucy Jane had a little solo, a *pas de deux*, as well as dancing the *Gopak*, the Russian folk dance, which they danced with the boys, and the new dance Miss Marova had choreographed for them herself. She felt the television recording could not come quickly enough.

10

Lucy's Decision

On the day of the recording the atmosphere at the ballet school was electric. Children and teachers alike were rushing up and down corridors with costumes, headdresses and sheets of music. Cameras and lighting equipment were in the main studio and electric cables were strewn everywhere.

Lucy Jane joined all the other children in the dining room, where they had been asked to meet after an early breakfast. She had her little mascot bear in a plastic bag with her ballet shoes, hairbrush and hair clips. She felt slightly light-headed. At last the pain of struggling to achieve perfection, of forcing her body to perform the difficult movements Miss Marova wanted, would be put to the test.

What she was most excited about was the *pas de deux* with Marie. This would really be her chance to show how much she had learnt, and give her an opportunity to shine. The first dance to be recorded was the *Gopak*. The children were hurriedly getting into costumes and doing their hair, when Miss Marova announced, 'I have news for you, the principal of the school will watch you perform today.'

The Russian children were tremendously excited about this.

Lucy Jane and the English children had not seen the

principal since the first day, when she had told them to be prepared to suffer. To them she was just a shadowy figure in black, and did not represent the impressive figure she did to the Russian boys and girls.

When Miss Marova had gone Karina and Anna said excitedly to Lucy Jane and Marie, 'Madame Krotchenova to watch. Wonderful! Principal of school much important.'

Marie and Lucy Jane looked suitably impressed but Miss Marova had become their mentor, their inspiration, the most important person in their dancing lives. What they didn't know was that the principal of the Hirkov Ballet School was one of the most influential and important figures in Russian ballet. She could make or break a young dancer's career.

When the children were ready, the small group in the Russian folk dance went into the main studio, which had huge drapes all round the room to hide the mirrors and black-out the windows. The studio was ablaze with lights and cameras, technicians and assistants, shouting and running in every direction.

Miss Marova was talking to the TV director, her hands expressing the movements of the dance, but the principal was nowhere to be seen, much to the Russian children's disappointment. 'Childrens,' Miss Marova said, her eyes shining with excitement. 'This is the director, Boris Tolstoy. You will rehearse the *Gopak* once for the director and camera, then we make video.'

The children quickly ran to their places to start, while the pianist practised the music.

Miss Marova walked up to the waiting children and said, 'Today is the moment we have worked many weeks for with heart and blood. Today is the day I want all pupils to give me all their heart when they dance. I want to see you dance with the joy of life. Dance to make your hard work look easy. I want you to make me happy when you dance.' She looked at them all in turn and said quietly, 'I love all you childrens because you love my love, dance. Now you show me you love me and dance with your feet and heart.' The children nodded. Anna had tears in her eyes and Natasha rushed to kiss Miss Marova's hand in a gesture of admiration and gratitude.

Miss Marova looked at the director, he looked at the pianist and the music began and the children started. The boys and girls moved from either side, their red boots clicking on the floor as they glided into the centre of the studio taking their partners as they danced. The boys with one hand on their hips, their other stretched out to take the girl by the waist and whirl her around. The children's feet neatly danced the

steps together and perfectly in time. As they spun, the girls' skirts swung out, their petticoats showing. Each child holding their partner by the waist, facing each other, hip to hip, and spinning joyously, their arms held out to the side.

'Stop, stop, stop,' the director suddenly shouted just as the children really thought the dance was going well. Miss Marova looked cross. 'What's the problem?' she asked.

'No problem,' Boris Tolstoy replied smiling, in perfect English. 'I want to watch the dance from the caravan and see it on camera,' and he left the studio to go down into the video recording van, where on small screens he could see all the pictures that each camera was taking. There he could decide how he was going to compose his shots and which camera would be used for filming which part of the dance.

The children were relieved that it was nothing to do with them. As Lucy Jane and Marie had not reached their *pas de deux*, they were still uneasy and exchanged anxious glances.

'I hope we get to the *pas de deux* next time,' Lucy Jane whispered to Marie, who was looking very pale and nervous.

'I hope we get it over and can go home,' Marie replied, fiddling with her white blouse and flowered headdress. 'These Russian peasant clothes are so hot. I'll be glad when we do the *Moon Ballet*,' she said. 'I don't like this one so much. But I love the chiffon dresses and pale leotard and tights for the *Moon Ballet*.'

'Let's think about this dance now,' Lucy Jane said, concerned that Marie would mess up their *pas de deux* if she wasn't concentrating.

Once the director was in the recording van and could see the children on camera, he asked them to start again. This time they got to the end of the dance, but made more mistakes than they had ever made before.

Miss Marova looked very disappointed. Lucy Jane and Marie stood shamefaced. Two boys had fallen over as they

did their kicks. They had to kick their legs forward while crouched and almost sitting on their heels. They swore in Russian and Miss Marova looked even more cross and shook her finger at them.

'Places,' the first assistant director said in Russian, listening to his earphones and repeating the director's instructions. 'If we have to stop please keep your places until we start filming again.'

Miss Marova repeated his instructions, and the children ran to their starting positions. Miss Marova walked to the centre of the studio, stood there a moment looking at the children, and then suddenly blew them kisses and made a gesture of support. The children responded with a thumbs-up sign and the music began.

The cameras recorded the dance from three different positions. One cameraman was on a crane and could move up and down, so he could film the children from above or below. A second cameraman was static at the far end of the studio, where he could see everyone in long shot, and the third cameraman had a portable camera on his shoulder and from time to time followed the children around, which was very disconcerting as he was often in the way.

Lucy Jane was determined not to let anything distract her, so she continued to dance her heart out.

Downstairs in the recording caravan the director sat with the principal of the school. Madame Krotchenova sat intently watching the scenes, her hunched body like a black insect peering at the young dancers on the screen. When the

children had got to the end of their dance she turned to the director and said in Russian, 'Put the camera on this girl,' and she pointed to a little figure on the side of the scene. It was Lucy Jane. 'Please, I would like the camera to follow her, I want to watch her more closely.'

The second time they recorded the dance, one camera was trained in on Lucy Jane. Luckily Lucy Jane wasn't aware of this and continued to dance her best. When the recording was finished the principal said, 'Please show me more of this girl when they do the next dance.' The director agreed.

Upstairs in the studio Miss Marova congratulated the children on their performance, and said, 'There is only one bit the director needs to do again, that is Marie and Lucy Jane's *pas de deux*. This is not because the girls have gone wrong, but the cameraman, who was walking between the dancers to film them, was seen in the shot.'

So the girls repeated their *pas de deux*. This time they danced with even more sparkle and energy than they had before. Lucy Jane felt as if her soul was taking flight. Her face glowed with the inner happiness that came with dancing well. When they had finished Miss Marova was so pleased with them that she wanted to hug them. But she just smiled and blew them a kiss.

When the children had finished filming the folk dance, they had lunch, then they changed into their next costumes. When they were ready they went to another studio, which was converted into a small theatre, to film the *Moon Ballet*. The costumes for this ballet, which Miss Marova had choreographed herself, made the children look so delicate they could be blown away. The floating, multicoloured pastel chiffon leotards and tights suited all the girls beautifully. The girls wore their hair loose, and it flowed down their backs when they danced, making them look exceptionally ethereal and pretty.

The *Moon Ballet* was much more demanding and technically difficult, so the children dipped their shoes into the rosin box and rubbed and crushed the rosin under their feet so they would not slip. As they waited they practised the steps or warmed up, doing *pliés*, *battements tendus*, *grands battements* and *jetés*. They still wore their leg warmers until the last minute, although it was a hot day, as the children found it easier to dance when their muscles were warm. Once the lights were in position and turned on, it became unbearably hot, too hot, and the children were relieved they were in flimsy costumes.

As Lucy Jane danced the *Moon Ballet*, she really felt she was a ballerina. The classical ballet movements and music made her feel as if she was living in another world. Once again they rehearsed for the cameras and again Miss Marova gave them encouragement.

As they danced, their feet not making a sound, their bodies graceful and perfect, Miss Marova looked on happily.

Meanwhile the principal was still downstairs in the caravan watching the children rehearse on camera. 'Let me see this girl again,' and she pointed once more to Lucy Jane.

The director gave instructions for the cameraman to show Lucy Jane as she danced. Then Madame Krotchenova said, 'Show me the girl's feet. Put the camera on to her feet and legs. I have seen the facial expressions and body.' So the camera trained in on Lucy Jane's legs and feet. The principal said nothing, but after a time she demanded, 'Get me Tatiana. I want to talk to her.'

The director, who was annoyed at all the interruptions, sent a message down to the studio to fetch Miss Marova. A few minutes later, a very worried-looking Tatiana Marova arrived out of breath in the video caravan. 'What is it?' she asked the principal.

Madame Krotchenova looked at her. 'Why didn't you tell me about this little one?' she said, pointing to Lucy Jane. 'And this one.' She then pointed to Marie.

'I'm not sure what you mean,' Miss Marova replied nervously.

'I mean, these girls could be as good as our girls. These girls dance like a good Russian dancer. Why don't they have a solo?' she finished.

'Well,' Miss Marova started slowly in Russian. 'It's only this last week that they have really become so good, and then it was too late.'

'I see. I must see these girls,' the principal insisted. 'Send them to me after the recording.'

'Yes,' Miss Marova said, thrilled that the principal of the Hirkov Ballet School, who was famous for being so difficult to please, liked Miss Marova's two young star dancers. Hadn't she once called Lucy Jane a little star? Lucy Jane had proved her right.

When the recording was over and Lucy Jane and Marie hadn't any more to do, Miss Marova came to them and said, 'The principal would like to see you in the little studio on the ground floor.'

Lucy Jane looked anxiously at Miss Marova, and asked, 'Why?'

'Just go,' Miss Marova said, and left the two girls to change and worry about what was to come. Then they hurried along to the studio, as quickly as they could, their hearts pounding.

The principal was at the far side of the studio, practising a little movement in front of the mirror. The girls stood before her silently, too frightened to speak. The principal looked at them. 'Take off your skirts,' she said to the girls. Lucy Jane and Marie took off their skirts and stood in their white pants and tee-shirts which came down to the top of their thighs. 'Please go the *barre*,' the principal demanded. The two girls obeyed. The principal asked them to do their exercises without their ballet shoes. As they danced she said nothing, just looked fierce and did not give the girls a word of encouragement. After fifteen minutes both Lucy Jane and Marie were sweating and exhausted from the tension, and their muscles were shaking from tiredness. They had worked hard since early morning and it had been an extraordinarily taxing day.

At last Madame Krotchenova said, 'I like your dancing very much. You can be good ballerinas. What is your name?' she asked Lucy Jane.

'Lucy Jane Tadworth,' Lucy Jane replied quietly.

'I train you at this school next summer,' the principal said. 'No fee,' she continued, smiling, 'just come for six weeks next year to study dance.'

Lucy Jane could hardly believe her ears. The fact that the principal liked her dancing and thought she was good, was better than any of her dreams.

The principal asked, 'Your name?' looking at Marie. 'You are good too,' she said. Marie was pleased but the full impact of the wonderful news hadn't really time to sink in, before Madame Krotchenova said, 'And you will train also.' Marie gave Lucy Jane a quick glance, both girls' eyes sparkled with amazement and delight.

'Go now,' the principal ordered, before the girls had time to speak.

Lucy Jane and Marie said a nervous, 'Thank you, good-bye, Madame,' and scurried from the room, bursting with excitement, longing to tell their parents the wonderful news.

They rushed to the telephone.

As luck would have it the telephone was free and Lucy Jane managed to get straight through to her mother for the first time ever. 'I can come back here again for no money,' she told her mother. 'The principal liked the way I dance, Miss Sonia will be amazed, and . . .' Before she could finish there was a great noise in the corridor and Annette was shouting.

'Come on, quickly, they're showing us the recording in the big studio now!'

Lucy Jane blew a kiss to her mother down the phone. 'Got to go, Mummy – I miss you, see you soon.'

When Lucy and Marie arrived at the studio the lights were turned down, and the film of the recording was just beginning. To their amazement there seemed to be an awful lot of Lucy Jane and Marie. The camera followed them whenever they danced. As Lucy Jane and Marie watched, their cheeks went redder and redder and they could feel themselves tingling from head to foot.

Miss Marova walked over to them. 'Happy, my little stars?' she asked, smiling. The girls nodded, too thrilled to talk.

Annette came over and hugged Lucy Jane and Marie, and when she said, 'You dance beautifully, Lucy,' a lump formed in Lucy Jane's throat. Annette was, after all, the best dancer in Miss Sonia's class. She thought of what Miss Sonia would say when she heard it was Marie and Lucy Jane who had been chosen to return to the Hirkov Ballet School, and not Simone or Annette.

'I think it's my bear mascot,' Lucy Jane said to Miss Marova. The relief after weeks of hard work and the amazing result, suddenly made her feel quite exhausted and tearful.

'No,' Miss Marova replied. 'It's not the mascot, it's dedication, Lucy Jane. It's dedication and hard work.'

Lucy Jane felt really proud. She had been 'prepared to suffer' as the principal had said when they had all met on the first day, and she knew now Miss Marova was right. The tremendous improvement was the result. It was not the mascot, it was hard work. She hugged Marie happily.

'We made it to the end!' she said. 'We can make it again next year. All we need to do is be . . . "prepared to suffer!"' As soon as Lucy Jane had said the words a wonderful feeling of happiness came over her. At last she was certain that she wanted ballet to be her career, and she was prepared to devote her life to the suffering and hard work needed to fulfil her dreams.